To My Son-in-Law
Malcolm Julian

1

SOMETIMES Tim Wallace felt that he was on a zig-zag path. For nearly a year he'd been influenced by the ideas of first one person then another. And he'd begun to feel that none of his friends on this side of town was headed in the right direction.

He was alone one Saturday morning in early December standing at the wide window of the apartment in the new high-rise building. If he hadn't looked at his watch he'd have thought it was early in the day. The patch of sky he could see above the street which ran in front of Pinewood Terrace was smoky gray. There were no clouds in the dull sheet that hid the sun.

Pinewood Terrace. Tim wondered again where they'd got the name for the apartment building. There were no pines, not really any trees. Just round puffs of some kind of cedar in stone urns on either side of the entrance.

He thought back to how he felt when they moved from the Cape Cod cottage over near the end of University Avenue. His dad had already left the faculty of Chapel Hill High School to be sales manager of Midwest Industries which covered forty acres south of the city. He'd been excited and thought the idea of living in Pinewood Terrace was great and his dad's new salary made it seem like the Wallaces were really moving into a higher bracket.

Tim hadn't been able to understand why his mother didn't want to move. He remembered what she said. Things like, "But my roses are just now getting a good start" and "I love the flocked wallpaper in the hall."

His father's arguments made sense to Tim even if they hadn't to his mother. Harold Wallace said they could afford to have flocked paper in every room and order roses from the florist every day in the week. And on his own Tim thought she should be glad there'd be no grass to mow and that someone else would shovel snow and clean windows.

Now as Tim looked out the fifth-story window the memory of the look on his mother's face was as clear as if he were looking at a snapshot of that evening. She looked sad and like she was already homesick. She bit her lip then said, "Roses grown by strangers won't be the same."

Tim turned from the window and listened for

6

sounds from the other rooms. He heard neither voices nor footsteps. *Mom's probably out again. Here it is — eleven o'clock already, I wonder why she didn't at least call me. She probably thought I wanted to sleep until noon.*

Now he didn't really know why he had wanted to get up early. There wasn't much to do. He walked down the hall and crossed the long living room. As he expected the kitchen was empty and the pad of orange notepaper was on the round table. It was open to the page where Marla Wallace had written "Gone shopping. Your spending money is in the usual place. Food in refrig."

She was gone so much it wasn't necessary for her to write a separate message every time. She just opened the pad to the appropriate page and weighted it with the cut glass rose basket, which never held flowers now.

Tim could have repeated several other messages without flipping the pages. "At committee meeting. Dinner will be late. Eating at Country Club. Raid refrig or use what's in usual place. Working at hospital. Be home at 4."

The money was under the copper coffee canister on the left end of the cabinet counter. *Five dollars. What am I supposed to do with it? Eat that much? Amuse myself? Or just get out from underfoot? But no one's here for me to bother.*

Tim decided to fix his own breakfast. He hadn't for a long time, but he knew how from the days when his mother let him and his cousin Dale camp out in the backyard and cook on the two-burner gas stove. He hadn't seen Dale much lately. The boys

7

never went to the same school, but were together a lot during vacation and weekends.

The few times after the Wallaces moved when Tim had called to see if his cousin wanted to go to a ball game or swim or just mess around, Dale had been busy. He had a job working evenings and parts of weekends in the car wash over in the new shopping center.

As the bacon sputtered and browned Tim wondered what Dale was doing today. *Probably working. I might go over and see later.*

He thought of taking his bacon and eggs to the living room and eating in front of the television set. *But there's nothing on but cartoons. And I'm too old to be caught watching — even if I do still like them. Besides Mom fusses if I spill stuff on the white carpet.*

He sat on the metal back chair and looked out at the balcony as he ate. There wasn't much to see but the lacy black iron railing. Then snowflakes began to sift and dance in the air. He watched them for a long time, first from his seat at the kitchen table then through the French doors which made up nearly half of the living room wall.

Tim liked snow. The way it looked and felt and the special feelings it gave him. Lots of good memories were connected with wintry times. Like the year he and Dale had been snowbound at their grandparent's farm for five days.

The boys' parents had been worried, almost frantic, when a strong west wind came up and began to pile soft snow into ridged drifts. They were in Indianapolis and didn't realize the storm front had

Tim liked snow. He enjoyed lots of good memories of wintry times.

edged through Chapel Hill until they reached the turnoff of the four-lane highway. By that time the crooked road Grandmother Springer called Groundhog Lane was drifted full at every north-south crook.

"Not a car's been down this road since two o'clock," she told her daughter. "The groundhogs haven't even ventured out of their holes in this blizzard."

"But do you have enough food?" Marla asked.

"The freezer's near to the brim and I have yeast for bread. And the cows still give milk and the hens lay almost as many eggs no matter the weather."

In the five days before the snowplow cut a one-lane swath to the farm the boys lived in a world of pure fun. They helped their grandfather with chores, but the effort didn't seem like work. They hauled buckets of corn and bales of hay on the sled that had been hanging on a spike nail in the barn. Its rusty runners were soon gleaming and smooth, polished by being pulled and pushed over hard packed drifts and under the weight of feed and first one ten-year-old boy, then the other.

They dug a cave under the eaves-high drift at the back of the chicken house and left a ledge at the back for a seat. They coaxed Gram into letting them eat two meals in the white light of the snow room. She consented only after they agreed to sit on a folded blanket and get up if their bench melted through its layers.

Little memories of that time clicked in Tim's mind making pleasant pictures. It was like turning a kaleidoscope and seeing bits of colored glass of many shapes reflected by mirrors so they formed patterns.

He recalled the snow ice cream they made by adding Guernsey cream, brown sugar, and vanilla to bowls of fluffy snow. *Gram always asked if we were sure we scooped away the top and dug down to the cleanest snow.*

He relived the night when the colt of Cricket, the riding horse, was only a few hours old. The boys went out with their grandfather before bedtime to be sure the mother and the baby were all right. The shadows of the coal-oil lantern wavered and danced and their feet crunched on the snow. The barn seemed warm in comparison to the near zero air outside. Cricket nickered softly and the cows across the stable chewed their cuds with a regular chomping sound.

Neither Tim nor Dale had been glad to see the big yellow snowplow round the bend at noon of the fifth day. They knew that they'd have more and more catching up to do if they were snowbound and missed any more school. But they didn't want the good time to end. In later years they kept hoping they'd be at the farm when a blizzard came. They wished that they could relive that experience. But it never happened again.

IT WAS NEARLY one o'clock before anyone interrupted Tim's thoughts. By then the balcony was covered with an inch of snow and the railing was frosted in fluffy white.

Tim had about decided to stay in the apartment and watch whatever sports program was being telecast when the phone rang.

Lant Hartley answered Tim's "Hello."

"Hey, Man! Ready to go?"

11

"Go where?" Tim asked. He didn't remember promising Lant he'd go anywhere with him.

"To find some action. Who knows where? We'll find it."

Ordinarily Tim went along with Lant's ideas. Almost anyone in Chapel Hill would jump at the chance. How many guys Lant's age had a custommade foreign car? Plenty had wheels. But none as fancy! And Lant didn't include many younger fellows in his following.

Tim rubbed the palm of his hand across his forehead before he answered. "Could I take a rain — or snow check, Lant?" he asked.

"What's the matter? Chicken about riding with me when it's slick?"

Tim started to say no. But for some reason he didn't understand, he said, "Could be. Sometimes on dry pavement you scare me."

"Suit yourself, man," Lant said and hung up.

Tim went back to the living room and sat down on the gold velvet couch. He didn't know what to do with himself. He could call someone and ask him over. But what would they do? Little kids built model planes or played dominoes or made snowmen. Girls gossiped or listened to records or something. But what could two young teen-aged boys do on a snowy afternoon for fun?

He had just decided to dash two blocks over to the drive-in restaurant for a cheeseburger and a milk shake when his mother came home. Her gray fur coat looked silvery with the powdering of snow. Her cheeks were red and a little wet. But her eyes looked tired and were lined with shadows.

"Oh, Timothy," she said as she came across the marble tiled foyer. "Are you coming or going — with your coat on?"

"I was going for sandwiches."

"Alone?"

"Yes. Why?"

"Well. I'm hungry too. Would it be all right if I made lunch?"

"Well, sure. Why not? You're a great cook."

His mother smiled. "I don't know how you can be sure. We don't meet at the table much anymore. But if you're sure you don't have anything you'd rather be doing — "

"No, I haven't," Tim said. But underneath he wished she hadn't been so willing to leave it all up to him. *Why didn't she come right out say it was foolish for him to wade through snow when she could fix cheeseburgers as good as any drive-in cook — maybe even better.*

He got the feeling, once in a while, that she had decided to give up being a mother. Sort of abdicated, like kings do when there are other things they'd rather do.

2

FOR THE NEXT three hours the apartment seemed more like a home than it had for months. It was almost as if Tim and his mother were alone in the world. The telephone didn't ring. The sounds from the street were muffled and almost too faint to be heard unless a person stood near the window.

Tim's mother worked in the kitchen until his father came home just before five. She'd added pineapple sundaes and tossed salad to their cheeseburger lunch. Then she decided to make ginger and molasses cookies.

"Snow brings out the country in me," she said. "I want to begin from scratch and make things. Like we did when we only went to a grocery once a week."

"I was thinking about the farm a while ago," Tim said. "Mainly about the time when Dale and I were snowbound at Granddad's place."

"I remember," his mother said. She was beating butter and brown sugar and eggs in an orange bowl. The wooden spoon made clicking sounds on the sides. "We brought a Christmas tree home that day. Dad cut it from the windbreak at the west side of the house."

"And Dale and I hauled it to the car on the sled," Tim said. "I pushed and snow kept falling down my neck from the branches."

"It'll soon be Christmas again," his mother said. "But we'll not have a tree from the farm now. Not with the land under water. And Gram and Granddad in Florida."

Tim asked if she thought his grandparents would always live in St. Petersburg. He didn't have to ask how they felt about the fact that their 120-acre farm was now a small part of the big Prairie Creek reservoir. He knew. They'd been sad and unanchored and kind of lost. Tim had felt the same way for a long time.

"Your father mentioned the idea of going south for Christmas," Marla Wallace said. "But I'm not ready to say yes."

"Any special reason?"

"Well, several reasons actually. But one's special. I *think* Gram and Granddad want to come back to Indiana for the holidays. They wouldn't come right out and say so, not wanting to spoil any plans your father has."

15

She didn't have to explain the last sentence to Tim. He knew how business and getting ahead dominated his dad's decisions. *He'd go to a conference or meet a client anywhere, anytime, even on Christmas Day.*

Tim spooned the last bite of pale gold pineapple syrup from the sundae dish. Then he glanced at the clock and said, "I think I'll watch *Wide World of Sports.*"

"If there's skiing or a track meet call me," his mother said.

As Tim came to the doorway he turned and asked, "Couldn't you just *ask* Gram and Granddad? And let Dad go if he likes?"

His mother was rolling the creamy brown dough with quick gentle strokes. She paused with the floured rolling pin in the air, "I've thought of doing that. And I may. In fact I'm considering saying — " She paused and smiled. "I guess I'd better not go into that. Not until I've done some more thinking."

"You worried about something?"

"Well, in a way. But it's nothing that should upset you. I should have come to a decision about this long ago and put my foot down. Run along! I'll bring you a sampler when my first batch comes out of the oven."

Tim wished in a way that his mother had gone ahead and told him what was on her mind. He wasn't a child. And he still was a member of the family even though each of them went their separate ways more and more. Especially his sister Clea who had her own apartment in Indianapolis and almost never

16

Tim wished his mother had told him what was on her mind. He wasn't a child anymore.

came home or even called.

Darkness came early that day. The snowfall dwindled to a few floating flakes but the clouds hid the sun. Marla Wallace came to the living room to watch the last quarter hour of the sports program, the segment which pictured a collegiate swim meet.

When it ended she leaned her head back on the ivory plush of the wing back chair. "I almost wish it would snow all night," she said.

"So Dad wouldn't want to go out?"

"Yes. And to keep anyone from coming. I'm beginning to unwind. I've felt like a coiled spring ready to snap and go in every direction."

Neither spoke during the commercial nor until the news program had been on for five minutes. A rising wind shook the French doors, and the golden balls on the Westminster clock whirred gently as their turning marked time.

"This would be a good evening for a wood fire. Want me to start one?" Tim asked.

"Well, yes. That would be nice. But are you sure you weren't going anyplace? I wouldn't want to spoil your plans."

Tim didn't answer. He went to the utility room for kindling and wood and had the same thought which had buzzed in and out of his mind a lot lately. *I'd stay at home if Mom asked or even told me I couldn't go out. Why doesn't she anymore? Like she used to? I bet Aunt Doris still makes rules for Dale.*

The splinters of kindling were crackling and tongues of flame were curling around the logs when the telephone rang. His mother talked until the early evening news program was over.

She was smiling when she came in from the foyer. "You're going to have company. Of course, if you'd rather go out Dale probably wouldn't mind."

"Dale? Is he coming?"

"Yes. That was your Aunt Doris. The roads are drifting and she's afraid Dale won't be able to get home from his job at the car wash. She's talked to him and I'm going to call and tell him he's welcome to come here."

"Couldn't I?" Tim asked.

"I'd better," his mother replied. "To make sure he knows I really want him."

"Why would he get the idea you didn't?"

"Well, Doris said he thought his work clothes might be too messy for us."

"That's no reason," Tim said. "We're still nearly the same size. He can change into something of mine. I'll call."

By the time Tim had convinced his cousin to come in spite of his dirty clothes, Harold Wallace was home. He'd taken two Chicago clients to the country club for lunch and a conference about a contract. Then he'd waited with them at the airport until the snow eased enough to allow for a take-off.

Tim heard his father walk to the hall closet. After a few minutes he came to the doorway and asked, "Your mother ready? Or is she still dressing?"

"Ready for what?"

"To go to dinner," Tim's father said. "We only have a half an hour to get out to Bittersweet Hills. And going's slow in this snow."

Mom didn't say anything about going out. And besides, she's cooking dinner.

19

Marla Wallace came from the kitchen with a long two-pronged fork in one hand. "Wash up, you two. The steaks are broiling."

"What do you mean *steaks*?" her husband said. "We're almost due at the Bainbridges. You knew that."

"No. I didn't," Tim's mother said. "I checked my calendar this morning. Carefully."

"But I didn't tell Miss Lawler to call you until eleven. Just before we left for the club."

"Well, she didn't call, Harold. Or did she, Timothy? While I was out?"

"No," Tim said. "I was here all day and Miss Lawler didn't call."

Harold Wallace's ruddy face darkened to a shade of purple. Tim started to his room. And his mother bit her lips.

"That incompetent — " Harold began.

"Now, be fair," his wife said. "Miss Lawler's very capable and you know it. There could be several reasons why she didn't get through. Other business calls, for example. And how many private secretaries work Saturday mornings these days?"

"Well. This is not the time to take care of that. Get dressed. Now."

"I can't, Harold. You know how formal Tracy's parties are. You go on."

"But what excuse will I give?"

"None. No excuse. I'll call and explain."

"Well, all right. I can't miss this opportunity. There's a chance I could lock up that contract with Bainbridge Mills."

Tim was surprised that his father hadn't lost his

temper and insisted that his mother go to the dinner. *He usually raves for half an hour when something like this happens to spoil his plans. I guess he didn't have time to get really worked up tonight. He might have missed making one of his big deals.*

After his mother went back to the kitchen Tim wondered how she really felt. Did she want to go to the party? Hate missing it, maybe? Or did she dread what his father might say afterward about having his plans spoiled?

The telephone and the doorbell rang at the same time, stopping the questions circling in Tim's mind. "I'll get it," Tim shouted to his mother. The phone could ring a bit longer. Dale was probably at the door. He'd invite him in first.

3

BY THE TIME Tim had let his cousin into the apartment the telephone had stopped ringing. *Oh, well. They'll probably call again,* Tim thought.

Dale Springer wasn't quite as tall as Tim but he was erect and agile and had a clear and direct way of looking at people. He grinned and glanced down at his gray twill trousers. "I'm not really a slob," he said. "But I took a guy's place in the grease pit for an hour."

"Forget that," Tim said. "I've got jeans and T-shirts. You might have to make a cuff, but so what?" He turned toward the kitchen and called, "Mom! Your favorite nephew's here."

"My only one," Marla Wallace said as she came to the door. "But I have a sneaky feeling he'd be my favorite nephew even if I had a dozen of them. It's good to have you, Dale."

"Thanks, Aunt Marla. It's great to have a place to stay. Mom said the roads are pretty bad."

"Did you have anything else scheduled for tonight?" Mrs. Wallace asked.

"Well, yes," Dale said. "We're having a Christmas cantata at church. And the first practice is tonight. But probably no one can get there except the kids who live right in Springvale."

After Dale showered and changed he walked to the wide windows in the living room. The drapes hadn't been pulled and the night was spangled with the design of many lights. The falling snow misted their brilliance and gave the scene a many-colored, shimmering look.

"You can see all over from here, can't you?" Dale exclaimed.

"Except what's back of us," Tim said.

"You still like it here?"

The words, "Sure. It's great," were on the tip of Tim's tongue. But could he honestly say that? For some reason it was difficult to be anything but honest with Dale. "Oh, some parts are okay, I guess. But lately — Well there are times — "

Tim's mother called them to eat and in a way he was relieved. *I'd like to talk about this to Dale. But how can I? When I'm not sure what's bothering me?*

The three watched television for an hour and a half, with interruptions. Mrs. Wallace asked about

23

members of the family and people she knew in Springvale. She tried to talk only during the commercials.

Tim answered the telephone twice. Connie Salyers called first and wanted to talk and keep on talking. She didn't call Tim often. Probably she couldn't find anyone else at home. He knew she'd been grounded by her parents after the second-grade report was issued. Tim listened to a lot of chatter and answered in a few words. Then he said, "I can't talk now, Connie. Someone's here."

"Someone more important than Connie — Timmy-baby?" Connie had a smooth way of working on a guy. She'd practiced a lot.

"Someone important," Tim answered.

He was in the kitchen pouring potato chips into a wooden bowl when Lant called.

His voice sounded funny, like he'd been asleep — sort of fuzzy.

"Changed your mind?" Lant asked.

"About what?"

"Getting in on the action," Lant said.

Tim could hear voices, and music. Only there wasn't much melody, just a kind of pounding rhythm.

"Well, I don't know where that is but I'm not coming."

"Whassa matter — chicken?"

Has he been drinking? Raiding his dad's beer again? Tim wondered. *Crazy guy.*

"I'm just not coming or going any place," Tim said. He didn't explain that he had company. *Why should I? I already told Lant no once this afternoon.*

"Am I spoiling your plans?" Dale said as Tim

24

shoved the round hassock to a spot in front of the couch.

"No. Why?"

"You've had two phone calls. That's why. You don't have to stay on account of me."

"I'm not," Tim said. "One didn't want to — Well, I guess she wants to go, but can't. She's grounded and couldn't find anyone else to call. And that last one — I told him earlier this evening that I didn't want to ride with him on these streets."

"Lant?" Tim's mother asked.

"Yes."

"Well, I'm glad. I'm afraid I'd have felt like saying no if you'd have gone with him."

Several questions flashed into Tim's mind. *What does Mom know about Lant? How much? Who told her?* He didn't try to find answers because of the look on Dale's face. It was almost as if someone had drawn a question mark on his cousin's forehead with a felt tip pen. *He's wondering why Mom said she'd only have "felt like saying no."*

By ten-thirty Dale was yawning and had even dozed a time or two. "I guess I seem like a real small-towner to you," he said. "But I can't seem to keep my eyes open."

"What's wrong with being from a small town?" Marla Wallace asked. "I am, you know."

"Well, I don't think there *is*," Dale said. "But some people at work make remarks. Like a few Springvale kids make fun of country kids. I think it's stupid."

"Stupid?" Tim asked.

"Sure. The farm kids I know are really keen. They are way ahead of me in lots of ways. Like handling big machinery and knowing about crops and nutrition and stuff."

"You're right," Marla Wallace said. "People put each other down for reasons that are unreasonable. If that makes sense."

"I understand," Dale said. "But I don't really let that kind of talk bother me too much. I know a few things — like when I'm sleepy. I'd need props on my eyelids to stay awake much longer."

Tim wasn't ready to go to bed. He'd only been up a little over eleven hours. But it would have made Dale uncomfortable if he'd thought Tim was turning in because of him.

I'll wait until he's asleep then listen to FM radio by earphones, Tim thought as he turned out the lights.

"I had a lot of stuff to talk about," Dale said as he doubled and thumped his pillow. Tim couldn't see him but he heard the soft sound of a fist thudding into the stuffed feathers.

"There'll be time tomorrow," Tim said. "Unless snowplows get through faster than usual."

Within a few minutes Dale's breathing was regular and growing deeper. Tim slid the plug into his radio and listened to music, real music, for a long time. It occurred to him that he led a kind of double life about music. When he pushes buttons in jukeboxes the tunes which came out were what almost all of his friends would have chosen. He bought records made by musical groups with strange sounding names. He rarely played them when he was alone. Why should he? The same sounds came from circling discs everywhere he went.

26

The FM music blotted out all other sounds and seemed to erase all sense of time. When Tim felt himself sinking into sleep he flicked the switch on the radio and pulled the blanket up over his shoulders. *That wind must be strong — and mighty cold to get around these windows.*

As he turned over on his right side he heard footsteps in the hall, a heavy tread. His father was home. Tim waited for the sound of the slam of the door on the hall closet. Before that his mother came quickly down the hall. He heard her say, "It's terribly late. Did you have trouble?"

"Checking on me again?" Harold Wallace said. His voice always boomed, day and night. But it sounded a little different this time. Sort of slurred.

"Sh!" Marla Wallace said. "Dale's here. The boys are probably asleep. You don't want to wake them."

That's not what she means, Tim thought. *She's afraid Dale will discover Dad's been drinking. And tell the family.*

Tim's thoughts were like pieces of a puzzle. How did his mom really feel about things as they were? The drinking? All the social fuss? Was this what was on her mind?

He was too sleepy to fit the pieces of the puzzle together. Once he thought he heard his dad's voice from behind the closed door down the hall. *He has to be yelling pretty loud.*

Tim pulled his pillow out from under his head and put it over his left ear. He didn't want to hear what was going on — not tonight.

4

THE SUN WOKE Tim the next morning. Radiance streamed in his east window. It seemed brighter than usual, maybe because it hadn't shone for three days. *Or maybe it's the snow that makes it so blinding,* Tim thought as he slipped out of bed to close the drapes. *No need for Dale to get up yet.*

Then he gave the other bed a second glance and saw that it was empty. He grabbed his short terry-cloth robe and went out to the living room. His cousin was fully dressed and standing at the windows.

"I didn't hear you get up," Tim said.

"That's what I hoped. No use for me to keep anyone else from snoozing. Look out there. Not a single track in the snow."

I guess the city sleeps later on Sunday," Tim said. "No milk deliveries or anything today."

"Not even the Sunday paper?" Dale asked. "Ours comes about the same time as on any other day."

"We go to the corner and get it out of a deposit box. Want me to scoot down for one?"

"No. Not especially," Dale said. "I'd just as soon talk."

"Name the subject," Tim said.

"Well, I can't help wondering. You didn't seem keen about living here when I asked you last night. Not like you did when I saw you at the family reunion last year. Or is this none of my business?"

Tim sat down on the end of the couch and stretched his legs out as far as they'd go. "I don't mind talking about it — not to you. But I'm not sure what to say. It's just a feeling. Like life's flat. Sort of a drag."

Dale whistled in low key and shook his head. "A drag? How could that be? You seem to be able to — "

"You might as well say it," Tim prodded. "I know what you're thinking. I do about as I please."

"Well, it does *seem* that way."

"It is that way," Tim said. "And six months ago I'd have said this was a great way to live. But now — it's like I was thinking yesterday when I remembered us being snowed in at Granddad's. We had a great time. But we had to go home and that was okay too. But I wouldn't feel the same about coming back to this apartment. Not so keen."

29

"I guess I *can't* understand," Dale said. "Home's sort of a hub to me. It holds our family together like spokes in a wheel. We go our own way sometimes but home is really the center of things."

"It used to be like that for us. But not here. You wouldn't believe how few times we sit down at the table at the same time. Then there's another tough thing. But I don't want to talk about it."

"Sure," Dale said. "That's okay. We all have private feelings."

"I know," Tim answered. "And I think you'd understand how I feel if I did tell you. But — it'd be sort of disloyal. There's still some family type feeling left in me, I guess."

"I hope so."

The boys talked about other subjects for nearly an hour. Tim suddenly realized he was being careful about his language. He had to keep a sharp rein on his tongue to hold back off-color words. *I guess I use them more than I realized. And Dale's face would sure get red if I let one slip out.*

Tim's mother interrupted their conversation by coming down the hall and asking if they were hungry.

A puzzled look came over Dale's face. Tim could read his mind. *He's thinking that everyone's hungry before breakfast. No one in Dale's family skips breakfast or gets his own. Aunt Doris sees to that. Like Mom used to do.*

Tim's father didn't get up until noon. By the time the boys had eaten waffles and sausage, gone for the Sunday paper, and made a trip to the convenience store for food. "We're so seldom here for more than one meal a day that I'm not organized about buying

Tim's feelings were in a jumble.

supplies," Marla Wallace apologized.

Dale's father called before lunch to say that the snowplow had cleared one lane out to the highway. "He's borrowing a pickup truck and starting in," Dale said. "He'll be here in about an hour — barring trouble."

When Dale placed the telephone in the cradle, Tim said, "You look relieved."

"Well, I am, in a way," his cousin answered. "Not that it hasn't been great to be here. But I have some homework and there's a family night at church. My Sunday school class has the program."

Mrs. Wallace called them to lunch but Dale didn't move. He bit his lip and said, "I guess that sounds pretty square to you. Or do kids in Chapel Hill still use that word?"

Tim didn't know what to say. Most of his friends here would think Dale out of step with the times.

"Don't look so pained," Dale said. "Some things in this world are supposed to be square. Maybe I'm one of them."

Tim didn't want to hurt his cousin. But he meant it when he said, "If square means level and straight, you are. And don't *you* ever change."

Big Harold Wallace came to the table as his wife served the tuna and noodle casserole. He spoke to Dale, asked how his family was getting along, but he said little more than that. His face looked different to Tim, sort of sagging. *But I haven't been this close to him for a while.*

Marla Wallace hurried to the door when Dale's father arrived. Tim heard her say, "Didn't Doris come?"

32

"No," Mr. Springer said. She mentioned it, but was afraid she wouldn't get back in time to fill the basket we'll be lugging to church."

"I'm disappointed," Mrs. Wallace said. "It seems ages since we talked."

"It could be a good thing I didn't bring her. If you two got started we might not get home before dark. And I'd just as soon not be out on these roads if the wind rises."

Tim's father didn't come to the living room and Dale's didn't ask about him. Tim wondered why. Had they had a fight about something? They used to be friends and even went fishing together sometimes.

As Dale came in his father smiled and said, "It was sort of quiet around home last night, son."

"Am I that noisy?"

"No," his father said. "But you have your place. And it was empty."

Tim glanced at his mother. He wasn't sure, but he thought she had tears in her eyes.

The Springers started to leave when Dale's father turned and said, "Say! It slipped my mind. And I wouldn't have dared go home and tell Doris I didn't give you this message. She's making mincemeat and fruitcake next Thursday. She wonders if you'd like to lend a hand?"

Marla hesitated, then she said, "Yes. I'll be there if the roads are open. I had a meeting that day. But suddenly it's not important."

The apartment seemed quiet after Dale left. Tim thought of calling someone, but he didn't know what they'd be doing. His father left for the country club. Tim wondered why, but didn't ask.

5

TIM WAS restless after his cousin left. He couldn't remember when he'd spent so much time in the apartment on a weekend. Looking back, the time didn't seem long, but looking ahead to the rest of the day and another evening made him want to break down the doors to get out. Actually, there was no need for that. No one said he couldn't go anywhere he wanted. Seldom did either parent ask where he'd been. He had his own key to the apartment.

Tim wondered if the library were open on Sunday. *I should know but I don't. In the old neighborhood it was. But maybe that's because it was near the college.*

He went to his room but didn't sit down or flop on the bed. He puttered around picking up things and putting them down — things like the halved thunder egg which showed a sunset in blue and gold. Rock collecting was one of the hobbies he'd dropped. His boxes of agates and tiger's-eye and chunks of quartz were stored in the attic of the house over on University Avenue. This egg-shaped stone with hidden beauty and the paperweight of polished Apache tears were the only pieces he'd moved.

Tim picked up his telephone pad and moved the number finder up and down. *What's the use of that? I don't want to call anyone whose number I don't know.*

He thought of his cousin. Dale knew what he was going to do when he got home. It was all laid out before him like a map. *That's the way it used to be for me. There was never enough time to do what came to my mind. Now I do about what I choose and nothing's much fun.*

Tim decided to go down to the Rock Cave and see who was there. Maybe someone could come up with a good idea for the evening. He took his rivet-studded denim jacket from the hanger, then realized it wouldn't keep him warm. It fit too tight to leave room for a sweater underneath. *I'll just wear my topcoat — no matter if Lant and the others call it squares-wear.*

His mother came to the door. "You're going out." It wasn't a question — only a statement.

Tim nodded. "Just down to the Cave. As far as I know now."

"Well," Mrs. Wallace said, "I guess your father and

I are going to the club. We'll probably stay for dinner and even longer if he thinks someone is a prospective customer. Unless I gather up my courage."

"Courage?"

"Never mind — now," his mother said. "Like I told you before, I've been doing some serious thinking. We'll talk about it soon."

"All of us?"

"Perhaps. If your father has time or cares to listen. Anyway, you and I will talk. We may be the only ones who are interested or concerned."

"You think I will be?"

"I do," his mother said. She looked straight at him. He could tell she'd been crying again. But she smiled as she added, "Two days ago I'd have wondered if you should be a part of this decision. Now I know."

Tim shook his head and acted puzzled. But deep down he had an inkling of what was on his mother's mind. The remarks she'd made began to go together. She was thinking about getting a divorce.

He couldn't sort out his feelings about that. They were a jumble, a tangle like the tapes on his recorder when the spool ran the wrong way. His dad was on this getting rich kick and was doing a lot he'd never done before — mainly drinking. And all the socializing and entertaining made the apartment either empty or like a restaurant — not a home. Would divorce change things for better or worse?

As Tim hurried downstairs one thing puzzled him. *Has Mom changed? Or didn't she ever like this way of living?*

There weren't many people on the street. The winter sun had been out a while but was setting behind a bank of gray-blue clouds. Purplish shadows were creeping over the snow-covered walks and streets. Three boys were building a fort in the empty lot across the street. *They won't be able to do that next year. There'll be another high-rise building on that spot by then.*

The windows of the teenage hangout, the Rock Cave, below street level were steamy. Tim couldn't see anything inside as he went down the half flight of steps except the misty glow of hanging lamps. When he opened the door clouds of smoke blurred his vision.

Tim unbuttoned his brown tweed coat and looked around. At first he didn't see anyone he knew. Then a voice from the back booth called, "Wallace! Come on back!"

The Conover twins, Kurt and Ken, were talking to someone Tim didn't recognize. Kurt scooted over to make room and said, "We were going to call you then Bash came in. Remember Bash?"

"You must be fogged or flipped," a deep voice said. Tim sat down and looked at the fourth person in the booth. He was a guy. The voice gave that away, and the bluish shadows on his cheeks. He couldn't have told by the length of the hair.

"Sure, man," Ken said. "Bash moved before Tim came."

After ordering a breaded tenderloin Tim looked around the room. He could see better now. Two girls sat in the opposite booth. One was Kelli Davis. She was in his first period class. He didn't know the other.

37

The twins and Bash left him out of the conversation. It was mainly about the scrapes they'd been in without getting caught. He wondered if they were exaggerating. Some of these happenings went back a couple of years and seemed sort of daring for ninth-graders. All the talk gave Tim the impression that Bash had been the ringleader.

Before Tim finished his sandwich, Lant came into the Cave. Tim heard Lant before he saw him. Lant had the habit of whistling a few bars from *The Third Man* theme. He was always a little off-key but this made his trademark tune a little more noticeable.

Lant came to the back booth and pulled a keg-shaped chair up to the end. "Is this place ever dead!" he said.

"That's the way you *look*," Kurt said. "What kind of a trip you been taking anyhow?"

Just then Kelli and her friend started to leave the plastic booth. "Wait up, Kelli," Kurt said. "Take a look at your old steady. Where would *you* say he'd been?"

Kelli's face was white around the mouth and nose. Tim could feel tension in the air. Why was Kurt needling Lant? He thought they were in the same group. And why was Kelli so upset?

"Let her go," Lant said. "She doesn't fit in my life. No way. And what I do — I do.

Tim expected Lant to leave. But he simply sat and stared straight ahead.

Kelli was part way up the long room when Tim called, "I'm leaving too. You girls want company?"

Kelli turned and nodded. The other girl said she

38

thought she'd go to a movie — or something.

"What's the rush, Tim-O?" Lant said. "I got better plans for you."

"Scrap them," Tim said. "I'm going home."

Kelli drew a deep breath as they stepped out on the street. She seemed to be shaking as she spoke, "I don't know why I keep coming back to this place."

Tim didn't know what to say.

The stoplight was on red when they came to the corner. They waited until it signaled "go" even though only two cars went through the intersection.

"I'm actually not that big a dope," Kelli said. "I *do* know why I hang out at the Cave. There's no place else for a girl like me."

"Aren't you being hard on yourself?" Tim said. He'd heard things about Kelli. But around some guys you heard the same thing about a lot of girls. True or not, you heard them.

"Maybe," Kelli said. "I guess that's the worst effect Lant had on me — made me feel — well, I don't want to say the word — not to you, Tim."

"Why not to me?"

"Oh, I don't know. You aren't like most of us who hang around the Cave. Like you wandered in the wrong door. And speaking of doors, here's mine. Thanks for the company."

6

TIM KEPT thinking about what Kelli said even after he reached Pinewood Terrace and his room. How had she got hooked up with Lant? And if he took her on a wrong road why couldn't she turn around and go the other way? *But that's stupid. I know why. Because of what people say. Because of the labels. Once they're hung on you, it's hard to shed them. Someone's always there to see that they stay put.*

As the TV warmed up Tim realized how Kelli might have drifted into a relationship with Lant. *As I did. He comes on strong at first.* He'd met Lant at a reception for new administrative personnel when his dad first changed jobs. Tim was still excited about the move and ready to think everything about the new life was great.

Lant's father was a vice-president in the company and Harold Wallace's boss. From that night on Lant seemed to assume that Tim was his satellite, that his role at Central High was to orbit around him. *And I guess I've done it. Maybe too long. Not looked around at other kids.*

For some reason that he didn't stop to analyze Tim got up, turned the sound knob of the television to low, and went to the telephone. First he dialed Bob Spencer who lived next door to their home on University Avenue. No one answered even after seven rings. *Where could they be? They always used to be at home on Sunday night.*

Then he dialed Randy Loring's number. After a few clicks a recorded message said, "Sorry, the number you are calling has been disconnected." Had the Lorings moved? *How many things have changed over there?*

Tim decided to call Rhonda Neal. "Maybe I'm asking for trouble. Rhon's been practically begging me to pay attention to her since she moved to Chapel Hill. Or is that different now?"

When Mrs. Neal said "Hello," Tim answered by saying, "This is Timothy Wallace. May I speak to Rhonda, please?"

Mrs. Neal didn't speak for several seconds. Then she said, "I'll call her."

"Hi, Timothy Andrew Wallace," Rhonda said when she came to the telephone.

"I thought your mother wasn't going to let me talk

41

to you," Tim said. "Am I on a blacklist with her or something?"

"Oh — not exactly," Rhonda said.

"You don't sound too convincing."

"Well, you know Mom. She still thinks fourteen's too young for dating. But you didn't call to ask me out, did you?"

"No. To tell you the truth I didn't," Tim said. "I was here alone and got to thinking about everyone over there. What's new?"

The conversation lasted for nearly twenty minutes. Tim changed the telephone from one hand to the other at least four times.

Rhonda explained about the Lorings. Randy's father was on sabbatical leave and studying at Oxford. The family had rented a house and the children were in an English school. "Most kids board there but Suzy and Randy go home nights."

Tim asked a lot of questions about old friends and teachers. "I know about the Owl teams," he said. "I check the papers all the time."

"That seems funny — funny-peculiar," Rhonda said.

"What do you mean?"

"Well, you live four or maybe five miles away. Yet you have to read about what goes on over here in the newspapers. It's like you moved out of the state or something. Don't you *ever* come to see *anyone*? We'd speak to you, you know. Most of us would remember you."

"Oh, you would, would you?"

"Sure. It's not like you're exiled or deported or something," Rhonda said.

"Sometimes I feel like I am," Tim said. "In a foreign country or another world."

"You don't sound too keen about things," Rhonda said.

"No. Not right now anyway."

"Well, I tell you," Rhonda said. "Just in case you've forgotten. University Heights is still on the west side of town. You come across the business district to the bridge, turn right — "

"I know. I know!" Tim said.

"And Tim," Rhonda added. "Don't be scared of *me*. I'm a big girl. I don't tag around after neighbor boys now. You're safe."

Somehow Tim felt relieved. Not that Rhonda's crush on him had ever really been a bother. She'd been cute as a little kid and showed signs of being more than pretty the last time he'd seen her. Now she sounded honest and friendly, not pushy like a lot of girls, or hard like Kelli was most of the time.

Tim glanced at his watch. "Hey, it's nearly ten," he said. "I'd better let you go. It's been great talking to you. I may get over there sometime soon."

"Well, like I said. We won't shun you or anything," Rhonda said.

Tim tried to concentrate on studying for a government test but pieces of conversation were all jumbled up in his head. Things Kelli, Kurt, Lant, the guy called Bash, and Rhonda said were like pieces of a puzzle that wouldn't stay in place or fit. He decided to go to bed and listen to FM radio. Music might erase the tangled thoughts.

But first he went to the kitchen, drank a glass of orange juice, and picked up an apple to take to his

43

room. Then he heard the front door open and footsteps came down the hall — a pair of clicking heels.

"Mom?" he called.

"Yes," Marla Wallace said.

"I didn't think you'd be home this soon."

"Well, I am. And I'll be here even earlier from now on," his mother said.

She came to the doorway. Tim could see that her eyes were sparkling. They did that when she felt deeply about anything. Glints of gold darted out from the brown, like a tiger's-eye stone when it was held up to the light.

"Something happen?" Tim asked.

"Nothing new," his mother said. "It's just that I'm up to here with one thing. A drunk's a drunk, no matter where they are — at the country club or in a cheap bar on East Second Street. Or if he's wearing a black broadcloth tuxedo or a suit with frayed cuffs and threadbare elbows. I'm not having any more of it! No matter what anyone says."

She means Dad. This is what's been on her mind. Part of it anyway.

Tim walked over and ran one finger down her cheek. "You sound exactly like my mom."

"Who've I been sounding like? No, don't answer that!" She took off her coat and started toward the closet in the foyer — which would have been called the hall in their home across town. Then she turned and smiled. "I just remembered something you said when you were a little boy — not much more than two years old."

She told Tim that money wasn't too plentiful in

those days. They'd made a down payment on the Cape Cod house and were buying furniture a piece at a time.

"Your dad was still working on his master's degree. I'd done some baby-sitting and saved my pay to get a beauty shop permanent. It seemed like it had been years since I'd done that. When I came home you took one look at me and said, 'Mommy, you look like some lady I don't know.' At that moment I wished I could wash the waves right out of my hair!"

Tim smiled and said, "Well, it's not that way now. Tonight you look like a lady I *do* know."

7

TIM DIDN'T see Lant at school the next day, but this wasn't unusual. Lant skipped a lot and they weren't in the same classes. When Kelli walked into fifth period English class, Tim thought of asking her if she'd seen Lant. He kept still for two reasons.

Kelli wouldn't be too interested in talking about a guy who'd hurt her. *And I wouldn't want her to get any ideas,* Tim thought. *Like believing I was making a play for her by walking her home from the Cave.* That's one of the things he'd heard about Kelli. That she didn't need much, or any encouragement to begin tailing a guy.

During last period study hall Tim looked around

the room. *There are sure a lot of kids I don't know, and haven't thought about meeting.* Getting to know people at University Heights hadn't been a problem. He'd always gone to school in that neighborhood.

A cold rain was falling at three-twenty when classes were dismissed. Tim pulled the collar up around his neck and ducked his head against the east wind. The needlelike rain particles stung his cheeks. He thought of going to the Cave but it was two blocks out of his way.

He heard music as he unlocked the door of the apartment. He was surprised that anyone was at home. *Or it could be no one is here. Mom may have forgotten to turn off something.*

The tall gold-based lamps were burning on the marble-topped tables at each end of the velvet couch. The music was coming from the room which Marla Wallace called *The Refuge.*

They'd had such a room in the house on University Avenue. Over there it was a wall-boarded corner of the basement where anyone could go who didn't want to be called to the telephone or to the door. Tim hadn't often retreated to this mahogany paneled room of the apartment. He couldn't remember seeing anyone in there, at least not his dad.

He walked toward the door, then stopped. *She doesn't want to be disturbed. That's the whole idea of a refuge.* So he went on to his room and turned his own radio on softly. He heard clicking sounds on the window. The rain had changed to sleet. Already the railings of the balcony were coated in ice. The scrolls of black iron were overlaid with frozen crystal.

Traffic on the street below was moving at normal

47

speed. The friction of tires hadn't allowed for any buildup of ice.

As Tim turned from the window his mother came to the doorway. "I didn't hear you come in," she said.

"I knew where you were. Working on some big project or something?"

"No," his mother said. "Just thinking. I have to talk to you, Tim. In here. Okay?"

"Sure," Tim said. He wondered if this thing she had on her mind was the divorce. *Or am I wrong about that?*

He sat down at the end of the bed and locked his hands behind his head. His mother sat on the edge of his desk chair and drummed her fingers on the Formica top.

She drew a deep breath and said, "The police were here this afternoon."

"The police?" Tim's mind grabbed for reasons. Had his dad been stopped again? Had someone robbed the mailboxes in the entrance like last month?

"Yes, I was ready to leave when they came," his mother said. "And after they left I wasn't in the mood for playing bridge. She paused and looked at Tim. "They wanted to know where you were last night at about nine, *and* I didn't know."

"I was here," Tim said. "Don't you remember? I was at home when you came in."

"I know *that*. But I didn't know what time you came back. *Or* where you'd been."

"I'd have told you," Tim said. "But why were they checking up on me?"

"Well, I'm not sure they were — on you, I mean.

48

They asked if Lant was here."

A light seemed to go on in Tim's mind. A lot of things had been arrows pointing to the fact that Lant was headed for trouble — or even halfway in it a lot of the time. He'd never actually smoked marijuana or passed any pills when Tim was around. But he always had money to spend — a lot of it really, and was great on treating people. Yet he had this habit of looking at his watch and saying, "Wait around. I have this guy to see. Sometimes he came back to pick Tim up. Other times he didn't show."

"Did the policemen say why they were asking about Lant?" Tim asked. "Or me?"

"No, they didn't," his mother answered. "Would you know?"

Tim bit his lower lip and shook his head. "No. Lant drives too fast and talks rough and he's in trouble at school a lot — about grades and being absent. But that's not anything the law would look into."

"But you *are* with him a lot," Mrs. Wallace said. "Aren't you?"

"Well, yes as much as I am with anyone over here. But he's with others, too. And I guess I don't really know what he does with a lot of his time."

"Which may be fortunate."

"Did the cops or detectives or whatever they were say they'd be back?" Tim asked.

"No, not definitely. They just said they were conducting an investigation."

"Didn't they say *routine* investigation like on TV?"

"No, they didn't."

In one way Tim wished he knew what was going on, but in another he didn't want to be mixed

49

up in the matter. He wished he could think of someplace to go — like across town or out to his aunt's. Away from the Cave and the telephone and the ring of the doorbell.

The telephone did ring a little after four but it wasn't Lant or anyone with news about him. Tim's father called to say he wouldn't be home for dinner or perhaps not at all that night. He'd made a quick trip to Indianapolis and if the freezing rain kept up until his meeting was over, he'd not try to get back to Chapel Hill.

"I wonder if the streets are very icy?" Tim's mother said as she came back to the living room.

"Doesn't look like it," Tim said. "Traffic's moving normally. Why? You supposed to be someplace?

"No. I was thinking about going over home. To our house."

"Why? Did the renters call? Is something haywire?"

"No. Not with the house at least. But they may be transferred and I thought I'd check and maybe visit a few people."

"I think we could make it," Tim said.

"Probably so. If the streets seem slippery we can turn around and come back. You do want to go?"

"I do," Tim said.

They drove across town and stopped at a drive-in restaurant. Tim kept looking for someone he knew while they waited for their cheeseburgers and french fries. There weren't many cars under the long plastic canopy. He rubbed the steamy glass and tried to see through fogged windows of other cars.

Streetlights reflected off the sidewalks when they

pulled up in front of their old home. Lights shone in the front rooms and the brass lantern at the front door was a glow of gold.

"Coming in?" Tim's mother asked.

"No. I don't think so," he said. He'd visited once when his dad came over to see if the new furnace was working. But he hadn't liked seeing other people in their old home. Even their furniture looked different.

"Well, I won't be long."

While Tim waited and listened to the radio someone pecked on the car door. He cranked down the glass and saw Bruce Gale who lived across the street. "What you doing over here?" Bruce asked. "I almost didn't recognize the car."

"Mom wanted to see the renters about something and then visit someone."

"Why not us?" Bruce said. "We're home."

It was nearly an hour before Tim and his mother started back across town. They'd have stayed later if the freezing rain bulletins hadn't scared them into leaving.

Tim caught up on the news Rhonda hadn't relayed. He saw Bruce's radial-arm saw in the basement workshop. He ate popcorn balls and felt as if he'd moved back six months in time, or farther.

Thoughts of Lant didn't enter Tim's mind until they walked into the apartment. And he dismissed the idea of calling the Conovers or anyone to learn what was going on. As it turned out he didn't need to make such a call. He turned his radio on low and forced himself to concentrate on outlining the Unit IX chapter, "Causes of the Civil War."

The musical program was interrupted by a news bulletin. "Local police have uncovered one source of narcotic peddling in this city. After weeks of investigation, five arrests were made this morning. Four who were apprehended were adults, one a juvenile. The adults are — " Tim reached over and flipped the switch. *They won't give the name of the underage kid. They don't need to. It all adds up — to Lant.*

8

TIM THOUGHT of telling his mother what he'd heard on the radio. She had been worried about the policemen's visit. *Yet she seems to believe I'm not in any trouble.* He decided not to bother her. She had enough on her mind.

He dreaded the thought of going to school the next day. Everyone was sure to be talking about Lant. News like that spreads in a hurry and would be everywhere by morning. *And anyone who knows me at all will associate me with Lant.*

He lay awake much longer than he ever had. He wondered why he hadn't tried to get acquainted with other kids. *It seems stupid now. Why did I think that just because Lant had the most expensive car and acted as if he were a big shot that he was my kind? I didn't choose friends for these reasons before we moved here.*

An answer began to emerge from Tim's sorting of thoughts, something like the way a computer processes data and provides a printout. Tim wasn't exactly proud of the result of his mental calculation. *I've been judging Dad because he's changed his ways. And even thinking Mom wasn't too interested in me, or making this place seem like home. But I've sort of flipped too. I've not been making the best choices either.*

He raised up, thumped his pillow into fluffiness, and wished he could turn off the switch in his mind and stop the circling thoughts. Finally he reached over and turned his FM radio on low. There was no disharmony in the music. It soon smoothed out the ridges in his thought and he didn't rouse enough to turn the knob before easing into sleep. He awoke to the sound of music the next morning.

His mother was frying bacon when he walked into the kitchen. "Morning, Timothy," she said. "No cold cereal for you this morning. How many eggs?"

"Two," Tim said. "Have you looked outside?"

"Indeed I have. The world's absolutely beautiful. Treacherous maybe, but still lovely."

"I know," Tim said.

"The sun on the ice makes it look as if the grass in the vacant lot across the street has been sprayed with silver and diamonds," his mother said. "I keep thinking of our yard at home. It must be a fairyland this morning. I can picture the rose hedge and the pussy willows and the barberry bushes."

"That's still home to you, isn't it?" Tim asked.

His mother nodded and smiled but her eyes were misty.

Tim had trouble finding sure footing as he walked to school. Salt had been sprinkled on some sections of the sidewalk but other parts were sheets of shimmering ice. A truck from the city street development was spreading something at intersections, but cars moved slowly and slipped sideways when the drivers tried to speed up.

Tim went to his locker and as he reached for his books he heard the first mention of Lant from behind him. He couldn't catch all that was being said. The clang of locker doors and the echoes of feet on tile floors cut into the conversation.

The first words were, "Old Hartley finally got it. Man! I'd hate to be in his shoes *now*."

Someone said, "Oh, yeah! How about all the times you've wished you were sitting in the bucket seats of his car?"

Tim wondered if his name would be brought up when a voice said, "Do you think anyone else was in it with him? Anyone here, I mean?"

"Time will tell," another said.

Tim's throat tightened as he headed up the ramp. He'd thought the whole thing was over. It hadn't occurred to him that anyone else was in on this dope thing. *Will they be questioned? Will I?*

He halfway expected to be called to the office and wouldn't have been surprised to have a policeman come to a classroom door. Kelli didn't come to class but Tim did see Kurt Conover in the cafeteria. He was alone, so Tim took his tray to the same table.

Kurt nodded as he took a bite of his toasted cheese sandwich. Tim waited a few minutes before he asked, "It is Lant — the one the police picked up — right?"

"Sure," Kurt said. "Who else?"

"Did you know — what he was doing?"

Kurt looked down. "I knew. And I could have been sitting in that jail cell or detention home right now if it hadn't been for my brother."

"Is that right?"

"That's right, Lant wanted us to do some pushing. The money tempted me. I could almost taste it. But Ken stopped me."

"How *could* he?" Tim asked.

"He went to our parents. I mean he brought the whole thing right out in the open. At dinner one night. Man! I wanted to fall through the floor. Naturally that ended our association with Lant. He still works on us though. Now that we know what he's doing."

"I noticed that he doesn't hang around you much anymore," Tim said. "But what I don't understand is — why do you still go to the Cave?"

Kurt rubbed his forehead with the knuckles of one hand. "The Cave's about the only hangout for kids. Most of the kids are what my older brother calls straight arrows like Ken. If we quit going then the Lant's will take over."

This made sense to Tim but he had another question. "Why didn't you or anyone ever warn me about Lant? Or give me a hint about what he was doing?"

"Well. We talked about it. I was all for giving you the lowdown. But Ken said to wait."

"Why? Wasn't he risking letting me get involved?"

"That's not the way he saw it. He said you weren't the kind. That you'd find out for yourself that you weren't in the same league as Lant."

Tim shook his head. "I don't know how he knew *that.*" Then he told Kurt what Kelli had said about him wandering in the wrong door.

"Things are rough for Kelli," Kurt said. "And they may never get better. She got involved with Lant in a big way. Then he dropped her — way down."

Tim felt a little better. Kurt hadn't suggested that anyone else might be questioned. *If he's not worried maybe there's no need for me to be scared.*

He went straight home from school. He wasn't in the mood to hear what was being said at The Cave. The apartment was quiet when he walked in, so he went for the usual note. There was a new one this time. "I'm at the market. Be back by 4."

Kurt Conover called and Tim was still on the telephone when his mother came in the door. Kurt wanted Tim to know what he'd heard that afternoon. "I went to the office, on my own, and told the principal what I knew. About Lant trying to recruit pushers."

"Do they suspect anyone else?" Tim asked. "Like me, for instance?"

"No. I don't think so," Kurt said. "Not you, for sure. But I think they'll keep a sharp eye out for signs of drug using and for anyone who might be peddling. The way I figure it, anyone not doing either doesn't have anything to sweat about."

Tim knew his mother would be curious or even worried about how his day had been. So he went to the kitchen to talk as she put away supplies and started dinner. The words poured out as if they were pumped by some kind of unchecked force.

Tim felt breathless when he stopped talking. It was like when he was a little kid and cried over stuff and had to sort of gasp for breath between sobs.

"You've been worried, haven't you?" his mother said as she crumbled ground meat into a heated frying pan.

"Yes," Tim said. "And plain scared. But you know something! One good thing came out of all this. I mean what Kurt and Kelli said about me not being in the same class as Lant. I just wish I'd found that out before school started!"

"Why, What do you mean?"

"Well. I took up with Lant because he was the only one I'd met. You know at that reception thing. It never entered my head to think he was in trouble. And I just didn't look for other friends — outside of his group, not even when it dwindled to a few."

"I suppose that's natural," his mother said as she stirred the sizzling meat.

"I don't know if it is or not," Tim said. "This is the first time I've moved."

"And I hope — " his mother said. "No! That's not what I mean." She stopped and turned her head toward the foyer.

Tim heard heavy footsteps.

"Your father's home," she said. "We'll take up this conversation later."

"Will Mom tell Dad about Lant being in trouble?" Tim wondered.

Tim wondered what she'd meant to say but he was more concerned about another question. *Will Mom tell Dad about Lant being in trouble? What will he say? A lot? Or nothing? After all Lant's father is his boss.*

Tim left the apartment as soon as he'd eaten. He had a report to make in science class and needed to go to the library. His father ate at home but left soon afterward. He didn't say where he was going. As far as Tim knew his mother didn't ask. Nothing much was said at dinner by anyone. Marla told about the letter from her mother. Tim asked if Gram said anything about coming for a visit, like at Christmas. Tim's father made no comment, neither then nor when she mentioned that the renters hadn't heard when the job transfer was to take effect.

In fact Harold Wallace spoke only two full sentences. The rest of his contribution to the conversation consisted of a couple of shakes of the head and two no's. Just as he pushed his chair back from the table he said, "You invited the Hartleys yet? There's not too much time before Christmas, before they sail for Europe."

Tim glanced at his mother. Her eyes met his. Then she said, "No, I haven't. I have some planning to do before I commit myself to a definite date."

9

TIM WAS glad the next day was Friday. Maybe the fuss about Lant would die down over the weekend. He knew that peddling drugs or using them wasn't right. In fact it was deep down wrong. But sometimes he felt that the users and pushers got all the attention, making the whole deal interesting or exciting to kids.

He knew that there were users over in Chapel Hill. There'd been some in University Heights too. He sometimes thought, *But why doesn't anyone ever mention the fact that a lot of us say no? Even when others make fun of us.*

As he walked to school that Friday morning, Tim

wished he could go a full day without hearing such words as pot and grass and speed — or any other term for junk.

As it turned out it was three days before he heard more than a few words about the trouble Lant was in or what caused it. He had chemistry lab at school that day and this kept him out of study hall. He decided not to eat in the cafeteria where news circulated freely. The sun was warm, so he walked three blocks over to the Fish 'n Chips eating place.

He thought two or three times of going to the first home basketball game of the season. But somehow this idea didn't seem so great. He didn't know anyone on the team. There was one player in his history class but he had quite a following and Tim hadn't ever talked to him.

I wonder who University Heights plays tonight? he thought. *I forgot to look in the* **Clarion.** He hurried to the library and scanned the sports pages. *Good! Muncie Burris comes to town.* He glanced at the clock and made it to the telephone booth in the hall before the warning buzzer echoed through the halls. As he dialed he wondered if his mother would be at home.

He was a little surprised when she answered. He crammed his reason for calling in two minutes. "I'm thinking about going over to University High for their ball game," he said. "I thought I'd call now in case you're gone when I get home."

"No. I'm here and will be all evening."

Tim was a little puzzled. His dad always made a big thing of Friday nights. Wining and dining customers usually.

"But," Marla Wallace said, "I'm going to your aunt's for the weekend. Want to hitch a ride? I'll leave early tomorrow."

"Sure! I want to go," Tim said. He didn't even think to ask if his dad was going. At first he wondered why. But by the time he climbed the ramp to the second floor he answered his own question. *Dad hasn't been friendly with Uncle Garry lately. Besides he'd be bored spending two days in a small town. But he didn't used to be.*

Tim decided to eat at the apartment since he knew someone would be there. Before sitting down to the table he called Bruce Gale. "I'm coming to the game," he said. "Does the B team game begin at 7:00?"

"No — " Bruce said. "They set it for 6:30, to leave time for half time stuff by the band. You coming for both games?"

"Yes," Tim said. "Maybe I'll run into you."

"Why make it a maybe?" Bruce asked. "I'll be at the foot of Ramp D at 6:30."

"Great," Tim said.

Tim rode the bus across town. His mother offered to drive him. "You don't need to," Tim said. "Not unless you want to go over there for something."

"No. Not now," Marla Wallace said. "Maybe next week."

"You mean to that Christmas luncheon at church?"

"Well, yes," his mother said. "For one thing."

Tim enjoyed the evening so much that he had to hurry to catch the last bus. He sat with Bruce during both ball games and talked to friends he hadn't seen for several months. He even went up four tiers

63

of seats and sat down by Rhonda Neal.

"I saw you come in," she said. "*And* I didn't dash down and latch on to you. Of course you realize that took a big chunk of self-control."

Tim grinned. "You're putting me on." Then he leaned back a little and looked more closely. "You're different," he said. "Your hair's short."

Rhonda nodded. "I guess I got tired of ironing it."

"Ironing!"

"Right. You don't think everyone's hair grows perfectly straight, do you?"

"I just didn't think about it!" Tim said. "Now I suppose you use fat rollers and gook to make it curly."

"How do you know about curlers?"

"I have a sister — or did have," Tim said.

"Oh, that's right. Clea. I remember her. She was so lovely."

Tim didn't say anything for a few minutes. He rarely did when Clea was the subject of the conversation. He didn't understand why she'd left home, not completely anyway. He just knew that there'd been some kind of trouble between Clea and her father. It got worse and Clea, his sister, took a job at the charm school in the state capital and left.

Only Tim's mother spoke of Clea. There was sadness in her voice when she looked through the mail and said, "No letter from your sister." And whenever Tim called his mother to the phone he had to disappoint her by saying, "No, Mom. It's not — not Sis."

When the game was over Bruce and Tim hurried to the cafeteria where the seniors were serving pizza to earn money for their annual trip. He was enjoying himself so much he forgot about the time. Tim was shocked into dashing to the bus stop at the corner of University and Talley when he glanced at the round-faced clock behind the counter.

The apartment was quiet. One tall lamp was lit and his mother had left a plate of pecan fudge on the end table. Tim ate one piece before he went to bed. It had been a long day and he had the feeling his mother would leave early to go to Dalton — very early. Days usually began at seven o'clock out there.

The next thing he knew the telephone was ringing. It was morning. He blinked his eyes and wondered why someone didn't answer. Just as he swung his feet to the floor the door to the entrance opened and he heard his mother say, "This is Wallaces."

Tim got up and hurried to the door when Marla said, "Clea? Oh — it's good to hear you. So good!"

Tim felt rooted to the floor. Maybe he was eavesdropping. And it could be that this call meant trouble. He had to listen. But he couldn't tell why his sister was calling by what his mother said. Her answers were short. "I see. That's understandable. Yes. I can do that. Gladly. Till then."

She stood with her hand on the telephone for several seconds before she turned and noticed Tim.

"I know that was Clea," he said. "Why — "

"Come to the kitchen," his mother said. "I need to put some food in the freezer."

"Is Clea in trouble or something?" Tim asked as his mother stacked cartons in the top compartment of the refrigerator.

"Oh, no," she answered. "Not at all. But she wants to see us — you and me anyway."

"Why?" Tim asked. "She's not bothered for a long time."

"I know. I know. But some hurts heal slowly. And — well, I think Clea's homesick. Not for here — she didn't live here long enough for that. Probably because Christmas is near."

"Then she's coming?"

"To Chapel Hill, yes. She has weekend after next off and wants to come to town and have us meet her at the motel. I'll be so glad — "

"Well, so will I," Tim said. "But why can't she come here? Is it because of Dad?"

His mother looked at him with a question in her eyes. "You don't know why, do you? You've never understood?"

"No. Not really. Just guesses."

"Well, maybe we were wrong, Clea and I, not to talk to you. It was her decision. She said she didn't want you to turn against your father because of her."

"But what *happened*?"

Marla Wallace glanced at the clock. "I told your aunt we'd be there at nine. I'm going Christmas shopping with her this morning. So let's drop this subject for now. All I want to say is that Clea couldn't be coming home at a better time considering what I have on my mind. If things work out you'll understand, and I think you'll be relieved. Trust me a little longer. Okay?"

"Okay."

10

A FEW FLAKES of snow were sifting through the air by the time they passed the city limits. "This is nice," Tim's mother said. "I always feel more like shopping for Christmas when it's snowy."

By the time they were within sight of the village of Dalton the siftings had increased and the road was snow-covered. His mother's small car slid a little when she pulled up from the four-way stop. "Maybe you should have driven the other car," Tim said. "Or have snow tires on this."

"I had to drive this one. Your father's in a parking lot somewhere in Indianapolis."

"You mean he didn't come home?"

"No. Miss Lawler called early this morning and said he'd taken off for Cincinnati. He wanted her to put some kind of prospectus on a plane."

Tim looked sideways at his mother. She didn't look worried. Or hurt. Her cheeks were red and her eyes weren't cloudy. *Whatever's been on her mind for a long time doesn't seem to be upsetting her now.*

They pulled on the stone-covered driveway at the side of a square frame house. Tim started to get out of the car. "Say! I just happened to think. What am I supposed to do all day?"

"Oh, I imagine Dale has some ideas to offer."

"But he'll be at work."

"No," his mother said. "Did I forget to tell you? Dale quit his job at the car wash — for the winter anyway. He's working part time for his father in the hardware store. They seem to have more business. Maybe because of Christmas."

The falling snow had muffled the sound of the car and Tim's aunt didn't know they were around until his mother knocked on the storm door.

"Oh, my goodness," Mrs. Springer said. "If I've looked out the side window once I've pulled back those curtains a dozen times. Then I missed seeing you. Come in out of the snow. Think it's too bad to go shopping?"

"Not for me," her sister answered.

"Now, Tim, about you. Dale's at the store. He'll come home for lunch. You can wait here and watch TV or go up the street — or whatever."

"I'll go," Tim said. He'd always liked to prowl around the hardware store, especially the second-floor storeroom. Things that didn't sell were carried up the steep stairs and lined up on rough wooden shelves. Tim had once asked his cousin why they kept stuff that looked like junk to him. He had to ask what things were, like cherry seeders and bread dough mixers and Daisy fly-killers.

Dale had smiled when he answered. "I can remember what my Granddad Springer always said when Dad wanted to throw things away. 'Keep anything long enough and it'll be an antique. Then someone whose money is burning a hole in his pocket will pay four or five times what it was worth in the beginning!' "

Dale and his father were carrying a television toward a yellow panel truck as Tim crossed the street. He stopped and watched them slide the cabinet through the back doors. Then Dale turned and saw him.

"Hi — I've been looking for you."

"We sure have," Garry Springer said. "We need an extra pair of arms today."

"I didn't know you sold TV's," Tim said.

"Yes. We've sort of branched out," Dale's father said.

"When the grocery store went out of business we took over that room," Dale added.

Tim hadn't been in the store for a long time and was surprised at how modern it was and at the variety of merchandise. "No wonder you're busy," he said to Dale. "There's a lot of stuff that would be great gifts."

"But you don't have to help," Dale said. "Dad wasn't serious. He hired a lady who comes in on Saturdays — but she has a cold or something today."

"I'd like to help," Tim said. "But I'll probably ask a lot of dumb questions."

"Well, that's one way of learning," Dale said.

The day seemed short. Tim was surprised when he looked out and saw the glow of the streetlights on Dalton's one business street. None of the three had gone home for lunch. Dale went out to the Copper Kettle, the drive-in restaurant at the edge of town, for hot sandwiches and frosted malts. Tim was so busy showing electric irons to a lady that he didn't know his cousin was gone until he came in with the food.

Later he said, "Did you drive?"

"Sure," Dale said. "I'm sixteen now. You know that."

"Yes. I guess I did. It just slipped my mind. It'll be a couple of months before I can get a license. It must be great."

"Yes," Dale said. "It is. But it's also a responsibility. Sometimes I get scared thinking my life is really in my hands — or in those on someone else's steering wheel."

Tim thought of Lant and wondered how he'd escaped getting hurt or killing someone — especially if he took the dope he peddled. He didn't like such thoughts and hurried to help his uncle carry a dishwasher to the delivery truck.

The two boys went to a high school basketball game over in Wayne County that night. Tim didn't know many kids but he had a good time. Being with Dale gave him a comfortable feeling. It always had.

When the boys returned to Dalton their mothers were in the kitchen making Christmas candy.

Squares of chocolate fudge cooled on one sheet of waxed paper and mounds of fluffy divinity dotted another.

"I thought you two would be worn out," Dale said.

"Well, maybe we are," his mother said. "We just haven't stopped to find out if we are tired or not. You boys want a sample?"

"I thought you'd never ask," Tim said. "But you didn't say. Why are you doing this *tonight?*"

"Because we always do this together," his mother said. "And we're together. It's that simple."

The boys watched television with Mr. Springer for a while. Tim began to rest his eyes during commercials and after a while he dozed and lost track of the story. When he woke up he couldn't make sense out of what was happening anymore. That's when he decided it was time to go to bed. He looked over at Dale who grinned and said, "Our night life's sort of quiet. Right?"

"Well, that's not bad," Tim said. "I guess I'm just not all that used to work."

The adults were in the kitchen when the boys went upstairs. They called "good-night" and went right on talking.

Tim didn't get to sleep for a while. He could see the moon through the long window even though it had climbed high in the sky. The snow had stopped in the middle of the afternoon. Now the light of the full moon on a frosted world made the night bright.

Tim could distinguish many sounds. People who thought small towns or the country were completely quiet hadn't ever been in either place. The difference was that you could hear the softer sounds when

71

the noise of traffic was absent. A dog barked hoarsely from across the street. The night wind whistled around the corner of the house. The steam radiators hissed when they were getting warmer and clanked when they were cooling. Tim could even hear his watch ticking without putting his wrist to his ear.

The last thing he heard as he drifted into sleep was the sound of voices from downstairs. He couldn't tell what anyone was saying and didn't strain to listen. Not like he did back in the apartment.

Somehow things were different here. Whatever was going on didn't seen threatening. *It's even a little like when we were snowed in at the farm. Safe.*

He went to sleep wondering if safety came from where you were, or who you were with, or how you thought. *Maybe all three.*

He had a crazy kind of dream sometime in the night. He was on a street where all the houses were squares of glass like giant ice cubes. He could see inside but there were no doors. Lights were bright and people wore summer clothes as if they were warm.

He wandered up and down getting colder all the time. He wanted to get inside since there were no doors. No one heard him pounding on the glass.

His shivering woke him. It took a minute for him to realize where he was. The night wind was causing the windowpane to shake and rattle. *The fire in the furnace has died down. This house is not steam-heated like the apartment.*

He reached down for the extra blanket at the foot of the bed. He was glad Aunt Doris had thought to put one there. He pulled it up around his neck and snuggled into its warmth.

11

TIM AND his mother didn't leave Dalton until after three o'clock the next afternoon. The boys were called to a breakfast of waffles and maple syrup — the real kind. The Springers drove out to Mt. Summit every April to buy a gallon of the clear amber product of Rutherford's sugar maple groves.

It was eight-thirty when Tim finished eating. Aunt Doris was busy sliding a roast into the oven and his mother was scraping carrots. He wondered why they were in such a big hurry to cook lunch when breakfast was barely over. Then he remembered. The Springers always went to church. *Like we did before we moved — and for a little while afterward.*

He couldn't remember why they stopped going —
if he'd ever known. The stopping began with missing
a Sunday now and then. The custom of going was
broken and the habit of staying at home became the
usual thing. Once in a while Tim had thought it
strange of his mother to miss. Now he was sure there
had to be a strong reason. Something he didn't know.
Another something.

Tim felt a little uncomfortable walking into the
sanctuary. He'd been here a few times before but not
for a while and had the sensation that all eyes were
fastened on him. It hadn't been like that when he
went with his grandparents. He'd visited West River
Church often enough to feel that he belonged. But
he'd never go there again. The churchyard as well as
his granddad's farm and hundreds of fertile acres were
under the waters of the reservoir.

As the congregation joined in the opening hymn,
Tim looked around. He recognized some people who'd
been in the hardware store. The lady who'd bought
the electric iron smiled and nodded. Once the service
began Tim felt more in place. Maybe it was the
music. Something gave him the strong feeling that
things were going together as they should.

After lunch the Springers, Tim, and his mother
went to the windbreak of evergreens on the back of
the lot. "The trees are growing and crowding each
other," Garry Springer said. "Maybe we can find
two nice straight ones for Christmas and give the
others room to spread out."

"Are we going to take one back to Chapel Hill today?" Tim asked.

"No," his mother said. "I don't know how we'd haul

it in. And anyway I'm not sure where I want to put it."

Tim happened to glance at Aunt Doris. She was looking at his mother with — well, tenderness. That's the only word he could think of to describe the expression on his aunt's face. He wasn't sure, but her eyes did look a little misty. Of course that could have been from the cold which reddened cheeks and noses and made eyes water.

"Well, don't worry about that now," Dale's father said. "You pick out a tree and we'll see that it gets to wherever you decide you'll be — be wanting it, that is, in plenty of time for Christmas."

Dale and Tim had time to try out one of the long bobsleds from the hardware store. At first Tim wondered if only little kids would be out on Hiatt's Hill at the edge of town. But half of Dalton, people of all ages, were taking advantage of the first real snowfall of the season. The air was clear and crisp and the fragrance of woodsmoke curled from the hand warming fire at the foot and to one side of the long slope.

The first sledders had packed the snow into a shining slide. The smooth and breathtaking swoops down the incline made the plodding, upward climb worth making.

There was just time for Tim to change into dry clothes before heading back to the city. He was stuffing things into a canvas duffel bag when Dale's father rapped on the door.

"I have a proposition for you, Tim," he said. "Now, remember you're not obligated to say yes. Just because we're family doesn't mean you owe me anything. It'd be the other way around. I'd owe you."

75

Tim smiled. "I know what you're going to say. The answer is yes. I'll help you out in the store — when you need me."

His uncle shook his head. "How'd you know what was on my mind!"

Tim shrugged his shoulders. "I don't know. Maybe because I was thinking the same thing. Or wishing it."

"Well, that's settled," Garry Springer said. "I've already consulted your mother. I can use you any time — even on Friday nights until Christmas. But I wouldn't want you to miss out on anything that's important."

"I won't," Tim said. "There's not that much for me to do over where we are now, anyway."

"Well — maybe that'll change," his uncle said. "You never can tell!"

Tim and his mother said very few words on the trip to Chapel Hill. Once she asked, "Enjoy yourself? Timothy?"

"I sure did. It was great. You know about me working in the store?"

"Yes. You like the idea, don't you?"

"It's great," Tim said. "Really great."

Tim dreaded going back to the apartment. He knew how it would seem. Big and richly furnished, and about as much like home as a furniture store. *And if Dad's home he'll probably be in a bad mood — like usual.* No sounds came from any of the rooms. One tall lamp was lit. *Had they left it on?*

His mother walked to the closet in the foyer. "Your father's home," she said, as she opened the door. "His coat's here — the one he wore."

Then she turned and walked to Tim. She put one hand on his wrist and said, "This is the time, Tim. I have to talk to him. About what's on my mind."

"And you want me to leave?"

"No. I didn't say that," she answered. "I just want you to know that this may be a long and loud and very painful conversation. And I'd like to spare your feelings, I guess."

"How about *your* feelings?"

"Well, they'll get bruised. That I know. But let me tell you something, Tim. Or make a confession. Grown-ups make mistakes sometimes." Her eyes twinkled as she added, "Or had you noticed?"

"I've noticed."

"One of the biggest mistakes I've made is in not having some things settled before I consented to move over here. I didn't ever like the idea. But it's not pleasant or easy to go against your father."

"I know," Tim said.

"You know a lot," his mother said. "Parents don't realize how aware their children are of trouble. I guess we don't hide things as well as we think."

"Do you — I mean will Dad change your mind about whatever you've decided?"

"No, no, he can't," Marla Wallace said. "That's why I've taken so long to come to a decision. I have to be sure this time. For the sake of all of us."

"When will you — "

"Tell you? That's what you're wondering. Right?"

"Yes," Tim said.

"As soon as I've talked to your father and can withdraw from the argument. I'll come to see if you're home."

"Mom, I'm not going anywhere," Tim said. "I'll stay in my room and turn the radio knob up a couple of extra notches if you'll be uneasy about me hearing Dad yell. But I'm staying here."

His mother reached out and touched his cheek. "I'm glad. That's what I hoped you'd say." She started down the hall, then she turned and said, "Tim, don't be scared. Of course I have to admit I'm a little trembly. But this is a move I should have made long ago — a stand I should've taken."

Tim forced himself to open his books and begin on homework, but his mind wouldn't focus on the reconstruction period after the Civil War. He didn't think his father would physically harm his mother. But — well, since he'd started drinking his actions were different and unpredictable. He either ignored everything that was going on or became angry over little things like who'd moved the *Wall Street Journal* or why couldn't his wife remember that he preferred to grind his own pepper at the table.

It was an hour before Marla Wallace came to Tim's door. But it seemed like forever. He was restless after he'd outlined his history lesson and felt like pacing the floor. In fact he did walk to the window three times. He changed the radio dials twice. He'd about decided to go to the kitchen and scrounge around in the refrigerator when he heard the familiar signal, two short raps — a long and two more quick taps.

"Come in," he said. His eyes riveted on his mother's face as she entered the room. She was pale but hadn't been crying. That was a good sign. One of his dad's tactics was to yell, and break her down into tears, thus ending any of her protests or attempts to reason with him.

"Well, Timothy Andrew," she said. "I did it. And I'm still in one piece. How would you like to move back to University Avenue? With me?"

12

TIM COULDN'T say anything for a few minutes. He knew how he felt but there was a tangle of questions and answers in his mind. The idea of moving back to the Cape Cod cottage was like going home — really going home. He hadn't even thought that this might be what was on his mother's mind. *Maybe when I get this all sorted out I'll see that she was giving me clues all the time.*

"I thought you'd be glad," his mother said. "I was so sure —"

"Oh, Mom. I am," he said. "It's — well the *greatest*. And I guess I didn't realize this until now. That's home. I mean, where I belong."

"I know," his mother said. "For me too. But why did you take so long in answering?"

"It was what you said," Tim answered. "Did I want to move back with *you*. Is Dad staying here?"

"I don't know," Mrs. Wallace said as she sat down on the desk chair. "It's up to him. I know the Bible says the man should be the head of the house. And a lot of people think the husband's job is the most important consideration. But I'm not so sure."

"You sound a little like the women's liberation thing," Tim said.

"Maybe, a little," his mother said. "But actually it's family freedom I'm for. Freedom from domination by *anyone*, and the right to chose *how* we live — by what values, I mean."

"I know what you're talking about, Mom," Tim said. "You don't need to explain." It was the socializing and putting money and things first. And the drinking and maybe missing church — or even other things he didn't know about.

Mrs. Wallace ran one finger up and down the grain of the polished walnut desk. "And I'm not asking your father to change jobs or move too far away to keep this one. He can make the decision for himself — as he probably will."

"When would we move? When will the renters leave?"

"That's one thing that brought me to this point. That and the long discussion I had with Doris and Garry. The renters have gone. The job transfer came through earlier than they expected. The house is empty and waiting. Would tomorrow be too soon?"

Tim grinned and said, "How about tonight?"

81

"Then you don't have any feelings against changing schools — before the end of the semester, I mean?"

"None, except to be in a hurry to do it."

His mother looked at the clock. "I'd better let you get some sleep. Tomorrow will be a big day."

She started out of the room but stopped when Tim said, "I have to ask. Did Dad give you a hard time?"

She leaned her cheek on the paneled door. "At first — yes. Then he seemed to realize that I wasn't going to change. And he sort of wilted. Just sat there and stared at a spot on the ceiling. I couldn't tell whether he was thinking about what I said, was too angry to talk, or was pouting."

Tim didn't go to sleep for a while. He looked ahead to moving and thought of calling Bruce or Rhonda. *But I'll see them tomorrow or the next day.*

Then he tried to put himself in his dad's place. How was *he* feeling now? In the old days Tim would have been able to guess. He and his father hadn't exactly been what some people called pals. And Tim wasn't even sure that he'd have liked that.

Now as he locked his fingers behind his head he realized just how much his father had changed. *I could count on him being a certain way then,* Tim thought. *I knew he'd listen if I talked or tried to explain my side of something. And he never put me down.*

How could a person change so much in less than a year? *Or has he changed deep down? Maybe he's just so wound up tight in the business that he doesn't see anything else. Will he ever?*

Tim was wakened by the ringing of the telephone the next morning. His mother was still talking when

82

he started toward the kitchen. She smiled and went on. "That's right. I plan to have our personal things packed by noon. Well — if you're sure the truck won't be needed there?"

Tim was dropping bread into the slots of the toaster when his mother finished her conversation. "That was Aunt Doris. She's coming in with the panel truck. To move us."

"You're not taking any of this furniture, are you?"

"Not unless *you* want something," his mother said. "These things wouldn't fit with our Early American scheme."

Tim spread strawberry jam on his toast as he asked. "Would it be all right if I skip school to pack?"

— "Well, I've been thinking about that. You wouldn't get much good out of going. Why don't you go over to the office. Tell them you're moving — and where to send your records. Then come back and help. How's that sound?"

"Great," Tim said.

He hurried down the hall and was at his door when he saw his father. Tim thought he had left. He was standing still, with his briefcase in his hand. "You're going with your mother." It wasn't a question.

Tim nodded. "Yes, sir."

"Well, that's as it should be — even if other things aren't."

Tim didn't know what to say. He just stood there turning the brass door knob — round and back, round and back.

"This place doesn't suit you either?" his father asked.

"No. Not now. Not everything anyway."

"I don't know how much you know of your mother's reasons. What she said about me or — "

"Mom's not said any bad things," Tim said. "And she doesn't have to explain her reasons. I know how she is."

His father looked down and cleared his throat. "Well, regardless of all that, one thing I have to say. I don't want you to go. This wasn't — " Then the tall man whose broad shoulders were now slumped looked at his watch. "I'll see you, Timothy. Some way. Some time. Take care of your mother — and yourself."

Tim watched as his father walked past him with heavy steps. He started toward the kitchen, paused, then left the apartment.

A kind of ache or tightening came to Tim's throat. *Was Dad really sad — or hurt. What will he do?*

There wasn't time during the rest of the day to think about the future of the Wallace family. Tim, his mother, and Aunt Doris were busy with the activity of the present.

Tim looked at his mother now and then to see if she seemed sad. Instead she was more like herself than she'd been most of the past weeks or months.

She hummed as she packed her favorite set of china and most of the kitchen utensils. She spoke of her husband in a thoughtful way. "I'll leave the rest of this pumpkin pie and all the snack foods. I can cook over there and Hal tends to scorch water." It had been a long time since Tim heard her use his father's nickname.

Tim packed his orange desk lamp with his clothes. The only things he wanted from the apartment were his radio, books, the thunder egg, and the Apache Tears paperweight.

Even though they weren't moving furniture they made many trips to the panel truck. Tim's mother took the portable television set and the Westminster clock with the whirling golden balls.

Most of her treasures were still in the Cape Cod house. Some were stored in the gabled attic.

The truck was loaded by two o'clock in the afternoon. After they carried the last load down and locked the apartment for the last time. Tim said, "I'm starved. Don't we eat on moving day?"

"Oh, my goodness," his mother said. "I forgot all about food. And I had sack lunches fixed! They're back there in the crisper drawer of the apartment."

"Want to go back?" Doris Springer asked.

"No. Hal might stay in enough to eat some of the food. We could stop at a drive-in and eat in the car. I look bedraggled."

"You look all right," Tim said. Her cheeks were flushed but she seemed younger. Maybe that was because of the faded sweat shirt and the scarf around her hair.

By four-thirty the contents of the panel truck had been carried into the white house with the charcoal shutters. Tim's aunt left soon afterward, wanting to get back to Dalton before dark.

She hugged her sister and patted Tim's cheek as she said good-bye. "I'll sleep better knowing you're here," she said.

"Thank you so much and tell Garry I appreciate the use of the truck. I'm sure he needed it.

"Well, he'll catch up," Mrs. Springer said. "Now

that he has such good weekend help."

Tim's mother switched on lamps and straightened a picture. "The renters took good care of things," she said.

"Are we going to unpack tonight?"

"You do as you like," she said. Then she shook her head. "No more of that! I dished out too much permissiveness. I think we should put our clothes away and let the wrinkles begin to hang out — some of them, anyway. Then I think I'll run down to the convenience store and get some cubed steaks and ice cream. Tomorrow I'll stock up." She picked up her purse and took out her billfold.

Suddenly Tim wondered. *What will we do about money?* But he didn't ask. Instead he said, "While you're gone I may go over to let Bruce know we're back on this side of town."

Before Tim's clothes were in place the doorbell rang. When Tim answered Bruce was on the front steps.

"Hi," he said. "Mother sent a welcome-back gift. Vegetable soup. Homemade."

"Great," Tim said. "I can taste it already. Come in."

"No. Not now," Bruce said. "We thought of having you over for dinner but Mother decided you'd be tired."

"Why *can't* you come in a while?" Tim said.

"Because I'm on the way to get some crackers for *our* soup," Bruce said. "The family's waiting."

"Well — Mom meant to go for stuff. I'll walk along. Okay?"

"Okay."

He and Bruce walked along University Avenue in the dusk of evening. The round globes of the street-lights shed a misty light. Many homes had decorated for Christmas. Some shrubs were dotted with minia-ture lights of gold. The bare branches of a redbud tree twinkled in a variety of colors.

Tim could see the lighted gold spire of the church over on College Avenue. The chimes in the tower of the University library marked the quarter hour. It was like he'd never been away.

13

THERE WAS no time during the rest of the week when Tim had to stop and think about what to do with himself. He was swept along by a stream of activity. There was work to do at home. He disposed of packing boxes and took out a broken storm window and replaced the glass. A sleety snow fell during the second night and steps and walks had to be salted and scraped. A tire on his mother's car picked up a stray nail and had to be fixed.

At school Tim felt as if he'd never been away. There were a few changes, three new teachers and several new students besides the ninth-graders who weren't there the year before. He ate in the cafeteria and it was like a reunion. He looked across the room as he slid his gray plastic tray along the stainless steel poles. So many hands shot up in greeting that he wasn't sure he recognized everyone.

The evenings were busy too. They ate at the Gales the second night and old friends called the third. No one seemed curious about why Tim's father wasn't around. Either they were being polite or someone had told them the reason.

About nine o'clock Thursday evening a question popped into Tim's mind. He'd finished a report for science class and was thinking about going to bed. *Tomorrow night at this time we'll be closing the hardware store.*

"Say, Mom," he said as he hurried to the long living room. "How'm I going to get to Dalton and back?"

"Well — I meant to take you, naturally, but when Aunt Doris left the other evening she mentioned another possibility. She said she might come in after school and bring our Christmas tree in their station wagon. Then we'll come after you Saturday."

"We?" *Did she mean Dad? Has she heard from him?*

"Yes. Clea and I. This is the weekend she's coming. Remember?"

"I forgot that in all the excitement," Tim said. "Does she know we're here?"

"No. I thought of calling her but decided to let things work out. You know Clea — she doesn't like to be pushed."

"What would she think you're — Oh, I know," Tim said. "You're thinking she might get the idea you

89

were twisting her arm to come back here *now*."

"Maybe," his mother said. "Of course this could be wishful thinking, but I can't help but feel that Clea wishes she'd gone to the university here."

"Not everyone's college material, Mom," Tim said.

"I know. I know. I'm just thinking, not shoving. And right now I'm going to drop all these problems and work on my needlepoint. It's my tranquilizer, I guess."

"I haven't seen you do that for a long time."

"No — I haven't," his mother said. "But this piece is a footstool cover and I'm going to finish it for Doris' Christmas gift."

Tim's aunt was waiting when he got home from school the next afternoon. The Christmas tree from the Springer windbreak was leaning against the railing at the side of the steps. He took time to drag it to the garage at the back of their lot before he went in to pick up his duffel bag.

As he turned to leave his room he saw a hump under his bedspread. *I don't ever do that bumpy a job,* he thought as he reached under to smooth the blankets. It was his mother's needlepoint. *She had to get it out of sight quickly when Aunt Doris came.*

That evening and the next day were a mixture of work and fun. By the time Saturday evening came Tim felt as if he'd looked at a million price tags and wrapped thousands of packages. His mother's car was parked in the driveway when he, Dale, and Uncle Garry went home in the delivery truck.

Clea opened the back door. "Come in, you men of merchandise," she said.

90

Dale grinned and asked his cousin, "Is that what we are? I thought we worked together in a hardware store."

Tim smiled at his sister and let her kiss him without making any objection. She looked great but she always had to him. Her black hair was piled on top of her head in a bunch of curls — which made her look older — but good.

Doris Springer asked the three-quarter segment of the Wallace family to stay and eat. "No. Not this time," Marla said. "I've fixed some of Clea's favorite dishes."

"Well, I like that," Tim said. "The prodigal gets feasted. How about me?"

"Well, little brother," Clea said. "You, as the Bible story goes, have been here all the time."

Tim grinned and he didn't say what he really thought. *No. I haven't. We've been away ourselves, in a sort of far country.*

He was surprised that he remembered so much about the story of the prodigal son. He'd studied it lots of times in Sunday school but never given it much thought afterward. Now — well it was like it fit his life. Was that how the Bible was? The truth was there all the time — waiting to be understood — or used.

There was a lot of catching-up talk during the ride back to Chapel Hill and while they ate. Nothing serious was mentioned until after the dishes were washed. Tim's father's name didn't come up until Clea put on her pink fuzzy housecoat and curled up on the wing-backed couch.

"You still have that old thing?" Tim said.

91

"Yes," his sister said. "I hope it never wears out." Then she looked at her mother and said, "We might as well get it over with. Why you're here. What happened? You didn't say when you called the motel."

"I know," her mother answered. "I wanted to wait until Tim was with us. There are some things he doesn't understand either."

"Like why I left?" Clea asked.

"Like why you left," her mother answered. "Shall I tell him?"

"No. I will," Clea said. "Actually it can be put in a very few words — now. At the time I'd probably have taken an hour or more to tell you. Like I did when I talked to Mom and Dad."

"Time condenses or distills things," her mother said. "Gives us perspective."

"Well," Clea went on, "it started this way. Soon after Dad took the new job and not long after we moved I went to the restaurant on top of the new hotel — on a date. And Dad was there. Not alone."

"With another woman, you mean?" Tim said.

"Right," Clea answered. "I was shocked and angry and left — not trusting myself to keep from making a bad scene. But later — well, I really told what I thought. I waited up. We quarreled. Mom heard us. She came out. And cried. And so did I.

"The point of the whole thing — besides my being ashamed — was that I hated what it did to you, Mom."

"Do you know what hurt most?" Marla Wallace said. "It was having you and your father quarrel because of my feelings. Nothing's as hard for me as a mother to bear than pain that comes to my children because of me."

"But you weren't to blame," Tim said.

"Perhaps not," his mother answered. "Except in this way. I should never have consented to move, feeling as strongly as I did that it was wrong — not for the right reasons. I should've trusted my instincts."

"Why do you think it was wrong?" Clea asked. "I'm curious."

"*Then* it was only a feeling," her mother said. "Now I know, by the results, that we made too drastic a change in too short a time. We couldn't handle the adjusting."

"Like what?" Clea asked. "I wasn't even around long."

"Like never being together as a family," Marla said. "Making business relationships the hub of the wheel. And for your father the greatest change was accepting social drinking as a necessary part of life."

"A lot of people think it is," Clea said.

"But I'm not a lot of people," her mother said. "And I have the right to disagree, don't I?"

"You do, Mom. You do," Tim said.

The conversation went on for over an hour. There was a short pause while Clea went to the kitchen and made hot chocolate and spread round crackers with a cheesy mixture. Clea asked how her father had reacted when they moved out. Then she brought up the question which had crossed Tim's mind. "How about money, Mother?"

"I have a little," Marla said. "You know your Aunt Mae left me a thousand dollars. But I'm going over to the university in a few days and ask for my old job back in the duplicating office."

"I know of a way I could help," Clea said. "If it's all right, I could move back. Get a job here."

Tim and his mother looked astonished. Then Marla reached over and patted Clea's cheek. "Oh, honey. That would be wonderful — and somehow right."

"There's one drawback," Clea said. "Like if there's a possibility that Dad thinks of coming back. He might not if I'm here."

"That would have to be his decision," her mother said. "That and other things." She looked at Clea then toward Tim. "What I mean by that is this. I'll never sue your father for divorce. I didn't leave *him*. Or the way I feel about him hasn't changed — not basically. I simply saw that all chances of staying together as a family unit would be canceled if we kept on as we were going. Tim wasn't happy over there. He didn't make friends that — enriched his life. We rarely saw each other. And I felt as if I was being pulled in four directions."

"Do you think Dad *will* come over here to live?" Clea asked. "I mean his pride's a pretty big lump for him to swallow."

Her mother smiled. "I know. But I wasn't just thinking about myself when I decided to move back. Or not only of you and Tim." She glanced at the clock. "Look at the time," she said.

"Why worry?" Clea said. "Tomorrow's Sunday."

"I know," her mother answered. "That's why I'm setting the alarm for eight. I'm going to church."

Tim mentally figured. *From eleven to eight. That's nine hours. Who needs more sleep than that?* "Call me, will you, Mom? I'm going too."

94

14

BY THE EIGHTEENTH of December memories of the months he'd lived in the Pinewood Terrace apartment had almost faded from Tim's mind. Faint traces remained, like wondering what his dad was doing and if he'd call or come see them. Once he saw Kelli Davis in a downtown department store.

Tim and Bruce went Christmas shopping that evening. He'd earned enough money working for his uncle and wanted to buy his mother Jessamyn West's new book. She'd heard Miss West speak at the university and was making a collection of all her writing.

The boys rode the escalator to the second floor

book corner. Kelli was waiting in line to go down. Tim almost didn't see her. She was just one of a group until she smiled.

He stopped and said, "Hi, Kelli," then he introduced Bruce.

"I wondered what had happened to you," she said. "You don't look like you've been sick or hurt or anything like that."

"No. I moved," Tim said. "Didn't anyone tell you?"

"No. I asked a few kids. The Conover twins didn't know. And Lant's not around."

"Well, I guess that's natural," Tim said. "It was a sort of sudden thing. And there wasn't anyone around that I knew very well the morning I withdrew."

After the boys boarded the bus for the ride home Tim thought about the conversation with Kelli. "I sure didn't make much of an impression in that school. Most kids probably wouldn't even remember I was there. And the few I knew didn't know what happened to me."

As the bus hissed to a stop, Bruce said, "Why don't you come over tonight? The air's cold and clear. Shortwave reception should be at its best."

"I'll see," Tim said. "Mom mentioned putting up the Christmas tree. She doesn't like doing it by herself. That's one thing we always did together — as a family. I'll call you. Okay?"

"Okay."

Before Tim and his mother finished eating their meal of salmon loaf and creamed peas they had two long-distance telephone calls. In the excitement of the news which came singing over the wires from Indianapolis and Florida they forgot all about the

"*I wondered what had happened to you,*" *Kelli said.* "*You don't look like you've been sick or hurt.*"

dessert of fresh fruit salad and chocolate chip cookies.

Clea called first. She said she'd given notice that she was quitting her job at the end of the week. When the head of the Charm Modeling School learned that she was moving back to Chapel Hill, he said they were opening a branch in the new shopping center and that she could help set up the operation and work in it.

"Well," Marla Wallace said, "that changes things. We'll not decorate the tree until she's here — either late Saturday night after you come home from Dalton or Sunday afternoon. In the meantime, I have my work cut out for me. The walls in Clea's room need painting and her curtains are a little dingy."

"I can help paint, after school tomorrow," Tim said. "No, I can't. I'll be going to Dalton."

"I know. I'll be taking you. So I'll scoot out and buy paint in the morning and do what I can during the day. You can help me finish later and move furniture back."

"It'll have to be moved *out* first, Mom," Tim said. "I'll get at that now."

They were moving box springs when the second telephone call came. Tim answered because his mother was boxed in Clea's room.

When the operator said, "I have a call from St. Petersburg, Florida, for Mrs. Marla Wallace," he yelled, "Mom, it's Gram or Granddad!"

"Oh," his mother said. "Come hold up these springs so I can get out of here."

They leaned the bedding section against a wall. As Marla hurried to the phone she said, "I'm not surprised to hear from them. They probably got my letter yesterday — or today at the latest."

The conversation didn't last much more than three minutes. Marla's father had never got over the belief that paying to talk to anyone was an extravagant waste. Tim couldn't tell much about what was being said by the one side of the conversation he could hear. His mother said, "Yes. . . . Yes. . . . You are! Does Doris know? . . . Well, I'll tell her. . . . Oh, that's wonderful. . . . Well, we can decide that then. Good-bye, for now."

Tim kept wanting to ask, *What does or doesn't Aunt Doris know? What's wonderful? Decide what, when?*

His mother sat with her hand on the telephone for what seemed like at the least a full minute. She was smiling.

"Mom," Tim said. "What was that all about, anyway?"

"Oh," she said. "I'm sorry! They're coming home."

"For good?"

"Well, I'm not sure about that. Neither are they or at least Mother wouldn't say. But they will be here for Christmas. Before, really. They're coming by train. You know how your granddad is about flying."

"I know," Tim said. "He always calls himself a well-grounded individual."

Tim almost forgot about calling Bruce. He didn't think of it until his sister's furniture was crowded into his and his mother's rooms. It was only eight o'clock. "Is it all right if I go over to Bruce's for a while?" he asked. "He invited me but in all the excitement I forgot."

"Certainly," his mother said. "Tell his mother the news if she's there."

It was nine-thirty before Tim crossed the street to go home. It was a frosty night. The shrubbery in front of the house wore glistening whiskers. The chimes in the bell tower over on College Avenue seemed louder than usual. They traveled farther when the air was clear. It had been the same way with Bruce's shortwave radio. Bruce had logged two faraway stations, one in Mexico and the other in Christmas Island way out in the Pacific Ocean.

His mother was drying her hair as she watched television. "I thought of calling the Silver Brush for an appointment," she said. "But tomorrow's already a full day. You hungry? We never did get to dessert."

"No," Tim said. "I had popcorn and potato chips at Bruce's. I think I'll go to bed. If I can find it in the jumble of Clea's furniture."

"I left you a path," his mother said. "But before you go, I want to tell you something. We had another telephone call. Not long distance this time — or maybe it was in a way. It was from your father."

Tim sat down in the platform rocker. He rubbed the heel of his hand up and down on the polished maple arm.

"He wants to talk to me sometime. Anytime."

"Is he coming here?" Tim asked.

"I think so. Sometime tomorrow. I told him I'd be gone for a while in the morning — buying paint."

"You mean he's taking time off from the office?" Tim asked. "That's a switch!"

"Well, it's not certain. I mean he could decide the work's too pressing or something."

"How do you feel, Mom?" Tim asked. "Do you want him to come?"

"I can't say now," his mother answered. "Simply because I don't know what he's coming to say. What's on his mind." She carefully tied a soft pink scarf around her head. "But somehow I feel that the pieces are falling into place. You know what I mean — Clea coming home and your grandparents being here for Christmas. *But* — we will have to wait and see."

Tim wasn't too sleepy to consider a few of the questions that circled in his mind. There was a lot of truth in one of his favorite songs "Windmills in My Mind." A lot of times thoughts did go around and around like the fan-shaped blades on top of the metal tower that used to stand on his granddad's farm.

There was more than one reason why his dad might want to talk to his mother. To give her money. Or to say he wanted to move back. Or *he* could be coming to suggest a divorce.

He raised up and gave his pillow a couple of good thumps. As he pulled the blanket around his shoulders his mother came to the door and whispered, "You asleep, Tim?"

"No."

She came in and sat down on the foot of the bed. "I should have told you. Your father wanted to talk to you."

"Why? Did he say?"

"Yes," his mother answered. "He talked to Lant's parents at noon today. They'd been in court. Lant was sent to a correctional institution upstate. For two years."

"For a first offense?" Tim said. "That seems stiff."

"Well. That's just it. It wasn't a first offense. It seems Mr. Hartley has managed somehow to get Lant out of other trouble."

"You mean buy him out?" Tim said.

"Perhaps. I don't know," Marla said. "Anyway, your father wanted to apologize to you."

"Apologize! Dad?"

"It doesn't sound like him. I realize that," his mother said. "But he distinctly said, 'I introduced Tim to trouble when I led him to think the boss's son was the right kind of friend.' "

"Well, maybe he did," Tim said. "But it didn't work out that way."

"No. And I'm grateful, deeply grateful," his mother said. "Well, good-night again. I'll see if I can find my way out of this maze, without stubbing a toe or skinning a shin."

"Good-night, Mom."

Tim was wide awake now. A question which had been jelling in his mind for weeks suddenly became clear and solid. *When does a guy really grow up and become able to make right decisions for himself? I thought the idea of the new job and fine apartment was great and went along with having Lant for a friend — for a while anyway. Then when things got all mixed up and Mom decided to come back here, I followed — went her way. How do I know for sure what's my way?*

15

TIM AND his mother left the house at the same time the next morning. "Why so early?" Tim said. "The paint store won't be open for over an hour."

"I know," his mother said. "But the supermarket will be, and the university offices. I'm putting in my application today."

"Well, good luck," Tim said. "I'll see you." He wanted to mention the visit she was expecting from his father. But what was there to say? It was on her mind. Of that Tim was sure. *And she probably knows I'm wondering what will happen.*

The air was gloomy when Tim left school that afternoon. Clouds of gunmetal gray were moving up and over the dome of the sky from the north. He made shortcuts through the alleys and across an empty lot to get home quicker to help with the painting.

He was surprised to see that the walls and ceiling were already covered with a pale rose paint. His mother was in the kitchen pressing the silky curtains.

"How'd you get all that done?" he said.

"I had help," his mother said. "Martha Gale came over with her roller and brush. The paint really flew around here."

"I can tell," Tim said. "You have splatters in your hair. Well, what's left for me to do?"

"Move furniture," his mother said. "And the fixture for one curtain rod is loose."

"Okay," Tim said as he started to his sister's room.

"Before you go," his mother said, "let me tell you what — or why your father came."

"Care if I eat while you talk?"

"No. No. The cookies are in that jar and there's milk and orange juice."

Tim's mother said that nothing much had changed — either for better or for worse. His father had left some money. He hadn't asked her to reconsider her decision. He'd wanted to know what they were going to do for Christmas. "*And* I asked him to eat with us, whether it's here or at Dalton."

"Do you think he will?" Tim asked.

"I'm not sure. He didn't say no."

"Did you tell him that Clea's coming home?"

"Yes. I told him. He didn't make a comment. His face flushed way back to his ears. Then he changed the subject. He asked what I want for Christmas. And you. What *do* you want, Timothy?"

"I don't know," Tim said. "I hadn't thought about it. Except to be glad we're going to be here. Say, what are you going to do while I'm in Dalton?"

"Oh, I have several things in mind. Like making a couple of white fruitcakes. And finishing putting Clea's room in order. She'll be here sometime in the morning. A friend with a car is bringing her.

When Tim's aunt came she and his mother talked for what seemed to him like a long time. He was in a hurry to get to work. The closer Christmas came the more business there'd be. He stood on first one foot then the other and leaned on the front door while the problem of who was to have the family dinner was discussed. Tim could tell that his mother wanted everyone to come to Chapel Hill. He thought he knew why. His dad would be more likely to come here.

Finally Marla Wallace said, "It's no more than fair that I have the dinner. Mother and Dad will be staying with you because you have more room."

"Well," Doris Springer said, "that's right, I guess."

"Then can we *go*?" Tim said. "Before one of you changes her mind?"

"Okay, Timmy," his aunt said. "Let's hit the Dalton Trail."

Tim's evening and next day at the hardware store were about like the week before, except they were busier. The store was crowded with customers at closing time and it was ten o'clock before they got home. It seemed like Tim had just shut his eyes when his uncle called them to breakfast.

His aunt cooked hot cereal and poached eggs

105

with a pencil behind her ear. She kept stopping to write on first one list then another. "Going shopping, Mother?" Dale asked.

"Well, yes. But some of these lists are work jobs. Things to do to fix up the spare room. For one thing — could we afford to put an electric heater from the store in that room? The folks are used to Florida and that corner of the house gets a lot of wind."

The store closed at six on Saturday and Tim's mother was waiting for him. She was alone. Clea had gone to the mall to look over the space where the modeling agency was being installed. Marla accepted her sister's invitation to stay and eat oyster stew. It was half past eight before they headed toward the city. The snow which had been expected all day began to sift through the air. It seemed to come directly toward the windshield, converging to a point.

"I hope it does snow and stays on the ground until Christmas," Tim's mother said. "But not too much! And I wouldn't want it to drift. I guess I want weather made to my order."

Clea called soon after they walked into the house. Tim answered. His sister said the work was much farther along than she'd expected it to be. "If I stay and help store supplies we can open by Wednesday. In time to be noticed by the last of the Christmas shoppers. Ask Mom if it's okay to trim the tree tomorrow."

"She says that's fine," Tim said. "I'll get busy and make a stand or hunt the old one in the attic.

Tim and his mother went to church the next morn-

Tim was surprised when his mother suggested that they walk.

ing. Clea had worked until nearly midnight and didn't want to be called.

A two-inch snow blanket lay over the city, but it was soft and fluffy. Tim was surprised when his mother suggested that they walk. "Scared to drive?"

"No. Not in this," his mother said. "I just like to walk in snow. I have my boots. How about you?"

They were at the foot of the church steps when his mother drew a deep breath and said, "It's easier this time."

"Easier?"

"Yes. I didn't say anything then, and perhaps relief has loosened my tongue now. But it wasn't easy for me to hold my head up last Sunday."

"Why?" Tim said. "Why should you — "

His mother touched his arm with her gloved hand before she started up the steps. "You know what Clea said about seeing your father with someone?"

"Yes — "

"Well, she goes here. At least she did."

"Mom. Are you sure? Who?"

"I'm sure. That's why I quit coming back. Oh, none of our friends. It was someone connected with the college. It would be better if you didn't know. Anyway, she wasn't here last week."

But Tim couldn't help wondering who it was, and if his dad ever came home would he come back to church? If so — how would he act — and feel if this person was around?

The Wallace Christmas tree was trimmed that afternoon. Bruce Gale came over and helped string miniature gold lights and hang gold foil icicles one by one on the fragrant branches. Clea and her mother hung the clear crystal balls and spaced bows of soft gold-tinted metal and ropes of gleaming tinsel.

Afterward Tim went to the early evening meeting of the youth group, who made plans to go caroling at several nursing homes on Tuesday night.

Tim and Bruce went to the Sweet Shop and the corner drugstore afterward. Bruce needed cartridges for his pen. Tim glanced over the magazines. There was a lot of junky stuff but he found a back copy of *Gems and Minerals.*

The Gales were at the Wallace home when the boys returned. Clea made caramel fudge which had to be eaten with spoons and Tim and Bruce made cinnamon toast.

"Say, little brother," Clea said. "When do you get out of school for Christmas vacation?"

"We finish exams Tuesday. Then it's all over for twelve whole days. That makes me think. Uncle Garry can use me right up to closing time on Friday. Only closing's at five that day."

"Well that's all right," his mother said. "But I wouldn't want you to be away on Christmas Eve."

"Don't worry," Tim said. "I'll get here. Even if I have to rent a team of dogs and a sled."

Tim was ready for bed when he thought of the hobby magazine he'd bought. That led him to let down the folding stairs to the attic and bring down the old suitcase and cardboard box which held his collection of gemstones. *It won't take long to put them in place on the shelves.* As he finished he thought, *That's one more thing back where it belongs.*

16

THERE WAS no time during the days before Christmas when Tim had to hunt for something to do. It was all laid out before him. School and work, Christmas shopping and friends filled the hours.

In one way he wished he could come home from Dalton every evening so as not to miss out on activities like the caroling and the last ball game before the holiday tournament. *But I can't do everything,* he thought as he packed his duffel bag Tuesday morning. *And the job comes first. Besides, it's not a drag — not at all.*

He was so busy for the next three days that he rarely thought about the one problem which nagged at his mind. Once in a while, like when he sold customers gifts for men, he thought about his father. *Should I buy him a gift? Will he come over for Christmas or before?*

His grandparents arrived in Dalton late on Wednesday afternoon. Marla Wallace met the train in Richmond and there was a reunion in the square white house that evening. Garry Springer and Dale and Tim took turns going up the street to eat and meet the homecomers.

A rush of warm air greeted Tim as he opened the back door and it was flavored with the aroma of frying chicken and fresh-baked rolls. The others were still at the table, nibbling a little and talking a lot. They took note of Tim right away.

Gram came to him with tears in her smiling eyes. "Oh — how tall! Too big to be hugged, maybe?"

"No, Gram, not by you."

His grandfather came around the table and seemed to shake his hand and slap both shoulders at the same time. "How do you like this weather, Granddad?" Tim asked.

"I like it," Mr. Gardner said. "It braces my legs. Puts zip into me."

After Tim ate, he and his grandfather walked back to the store. When they returned Marla Wallace had left for Chapel Hill and her mother had gone to bed. Dale, Tim, and the two men talked for over an hour. That's when Mr. Gardner revealed that they were coming back to Indiana to live. "No need to make aliens of ourselves just because one parcel of land is under water. There's other good soil around in this neck of the woods."

"Are you going to farm again?" Tim asked.

"Not on a big scale. But I'd like five or six acres or maybe more. I could do a little berrying. Do you know what Mama paid for raspberries the other day! Sixty-five cents for one small can! You'd think they were going out of style."

Tim's uncle took him home early on Christmas Eve, leaving Dalton promptly at five o'clock. "I hate to drag you away. I know everyone's going to the program at church," Tim said.

"So am I," his uncle said. "I have plenty of time. As a matter of fact I *have* to go to Chapel Hill to pick up the treats now that there's no grocery in our little town."

Most of Sunday's snow was gone but more began to fall as they neared the city limits. The shrubs in front of the Wallace house wore a topping of white. It glistened in the light of the brass lantern.

Tim started up the steps with his packages. He'd bought Clea a small crystal lamp for her nightstand. And at the last minute he decided he might as well get something for his dad — just in case he came home. Tim chose a compass for his dad's car which had about every other accessory available.

"If Clea's home she'll try to guess what's in this one package. I'll put it in the garage for now."

His mother's car was gone but that didn't mean she wasn't at home. Clea could be using it. *Or Mom could have made a last-minute trip to the grocery.* He went in the back door. Something was simmering on the stove. Escaping steam jiggled the orange-enameled lid now and then.

Tim sat down to take off his boots. As he raised up

he heard the squeak the platform rocker made when someone got up or shifted position.

"Mom?"

"I'm the only one who's here, Tim," his father answered. For a minute, or maybe less, Tim felt as if he'd grown roots. He couldn't get up.

Then he took a deep breath and shed his brown corduroy coat as he walked to the door.

His father had the *Evening Clarion* on his lap. He wasn't wearing his suit coat. And the knot of his black tie was loosened at the collar of his white shirt. He wasn't wearing shoes. He looked at home.

"Your mother's gone to the market," Harold Wallace said. "She decided one pint of oysters wasn't enough for dressing."

"I see," Tim said. "Is Clea here?"

"No. She was. And she'll be back to eat. I think she's shopping for a last-minute gift."

Questions that Tim couldn't ask seemed to tie his tongue. He didn't know what to say.

"Sit down, will you, Tim?" his father said. "I think your mother left for a purpose. So I could try to make you understand how things are in my mind. She did the same thing when Clea came home at four. *Then* your mother went to get an extra string of lights or something."

Tim sat down on the end of the couch. He didn't know what his father was going to say. He just hoped whatever it was wouldn't spoil things.

"Like I said," Harold Wallace began, "I talked to Clea. It wasn't easy — for either of us. We'd cut deep gashes in our relationship with the sharp edge of angry words."

Tim couldn't keep from smiling. "You sound like an English teacher now," he said.

"Maybe I am at the root of me. The economic minor thing could be only an offshot — a grafting," Mr. Wallace said. "But I want you to know that there's peace between your sister and me now. Do you think you and I can get back to where we were?"

Tim didn't really know how to answer. He hadn't fought with his father. They'd just grown apart. He surprised himself by blurting out, "Are you going to stay here?"

"Any objections?"

"No," Tim said. "Not from me. Not if it's all right with Mom."

"It is. You can thank God for that," his father said. His voice seemed to quiver. Tim looked at him in a new way — with a different feeling.

"Do you know what I think, Tim?" his father went on. "I think your mother knew what would happen if she moved back here. Sometimes I think she has a sixth sense about such things. Like something told her this was the only way to keep the family together."

Tim remembered having the same kind of feeling. "You may be right," he said. "Like the day we moved. I kept watching her face — to see if she was sad or upset. But she wasn't."

His father pounded a doubled up fist on the arm of a chair. "When I think of what I did to all of you — Because of a chance to move several income brackets up the economic ladder, I fell way down as an individual."

"Well," Tim said. "I guess we all make mistakes.

Mom says she was wrong to be in such a big rush to consent to move. She thinks she was weak."

"I know," his father said. "She told me. Well, there's one more point I want to make. I was shocked when she told me she was moving out of the apartment. I began to step off my ambition escalator then. But my mind was actually made up for me when the Hartleys came to the office from court. I realized that what happened to Lant could have happened to you — if you'd have gone along with your group — as I did with my new one."

The room was quiet for a few minutes. The gold lights on the Christmas tree were reflected in the crystal balls.

"Say," Tim's father said. "I forgot. We're supposed to start frying hamburgers. How was it? Did you fry or did I?"

"You did," Tim said. "I pressed the meat into the mould. But could that wait a couple of minutes? I have a package in the garage. I'd like to smuggle it into my room before Clea gets home."

The backyard was covered with snow as Tim hurried to the garage and the soft flakes were still sifting through the air. He could see them in the light that shone from the black iron lamppost. As he started toward the house he heard the music from the library tower. The chimes rang out the carol, "Silent Night." He stood and listened and the words ran through his mind, especially, "All is calm, all is bright."

The Wallaces were a little uncomfortable at dinner. They avoided talking about the past or anything serious. Tim could sense that each was trying to get back on the old footing without talking about the time when anyone had taken wrong steps.

As his mother began to clear the table Hal Wallace said, "Is it time to bring the turkey in from the garage?"

"Yes," Marla said. "It's partly thawed by now and should be all the way by morning." She made room on the end of the cabinet and spread newspapers to absorb the moisture from the melting.

Tim noticed that his father kept glancing at his watch. Was this a habit? Surely he didn't have to take care of business tonight?

"What time will the church service be over?" Tim's father asked as his mother came into the living room.

"You mean out at Dalton?" she said. "Why?"

"Well, I have some things to explain to your folks, and try to rectify," Hal said. "Especially as far as Garry is concerned."

"I see," Marla said. "You mean you're thinking about going out there tonight?"

"Yes. I'd like to. Otherwise tomorrow might be shadowed by strain, for all of us as well as for me."

"Want me to go along?"

"Well, I'm not against your going," Tim's father said. "But this is something I should do myself."

"I understand. But go carefully."

As Hal walked toward the hall closet he stopped and rubbed his knuckles down Marla's cheek. "Do you know something! That's one of the things I missed — having you tell me to go carefully. I may not have paid attention to your words, but I missed hearing them."

After he pulled away from across the street, Clea

116

asked, "Why does he want to see Uncle Garry — why him especially?"

"It's this," her mother said. "When things began to go wrong, your uncle tried to talk to him. He didn't listen and resentment grew into alienation."

Tim turned on the television to watch the Christmas Eve special. As it warmed up, he said, "It'll take courage. For Dad, I mean. To walk in and face your family."

"I know," his mother said.

Tim began to nod before the hour-long musical was over. "I think I'll go to bed," he said. "After I wrap a couple of things."

His mother followed him to the doorway of his room. "Feel better, Tim?"

"Yes, Mom. Things seem — well *right*. Sometimes I wondered if they ever could again."

"Fine," his mother said. "Good-night, Timothy Andrew."

He heard her singing as she stopped at the hall closet, probably for gifts to put under the tree. The words, "All is calm, all is bright," floated into his room and he experienced a warmth he had not felt for many months.

No matter what packages he found under the tree in the morning, he knew what he'd like best — the gift of being at home.

The Author

Dorothy Hamilton was born in Delaware County, Indiana, where she still lives. She received her elementary and secondary education in the schools of Cowan and Muncie, Indiana. She attended Ball State University, Muncie, and has taken work by correspondence from Indiana University, Bloomington, Indiana. She has attended professional writing courses, first as a student and later as an instructor.

Mrs. Hamilton grew up in the Methodist Church and participated in numerous school, community, and church activities until the youngest of her seven children was married.

Then she sensed that the Lord was leading her to become a private tutor. This service has become a mission of love. Several hundred girls and boys have come to Mrs. Hamilton for gentle encouragement, for renewal of self-esteem, and to learn to work.

The experiences of motherhood and tutoring have inspired Mrs. Hamilton in much of her writing.

Seven of her short stories have appeared in quarterlies and one was nominated for the American Literary Anthology. Since 1967 she has had fifty serials published, more than four dozen short stories, and several articles in religious magazines. She has also written for radio and newspapers.

Mrs. Hamilton is author of a growing shelf of books: *Anita's Choice, Christmas for Holly, Charco, The Killdeer, Tony Savala, Jim Musco, Settled Furrows, Kerry, The Blue Caboose, Mindy, The Quail, and Jason.*